WHAT DO YOU DO WHEN ALIENS KIDNAP YOUR CAT?

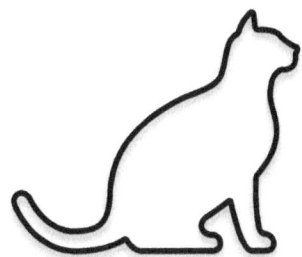

by Joseph R Gurner

Published by Joseph R Gurner

©2025 Joseph R Gurner

Original manuscript draft: ©July 2017

ISBN: 979-8-9988956-0-9

1st Test Printing: April 2025
1st Mass Printing: May 2025

Printing by lulu.com

Front and Back Cover Design by Joseph R Gurner
Clip art used includes: Stock cat silhouettes in Apple Pages, UFO
clip art - public domain (origin unknown), starry night background -
public domain (origin unknown).

Dedicated to my wonderful wife, Anita,
who is always happy to support my crazy endeavors.

Many, many, many thanks to David and Amelia, whose encouragement, support, critique, cats, dogs - and most importantly, friendship - helped make this possible.

Just Before The Beginning Of It All

Zev took to the sky.

The ground fell away beneath him. He knew any pursuit would probably be too far behind to make any difference, but he glanced back anyway. All he saw was the receding world below and the small pod containing four Methens trailing behind. He couldn't see them. The pod was windowless. But he knew they were there, scared from their ordeal, grateful to still be alive and thrilled at the prospect of the freedom that lay ahead for them.

Zev turned his head back to the sky. The ruddy red of the sky began to darken as he rose higher and higher into the atmosphere, his body cutting through the thin air. If anyone had been around to see, he would have been truly an impressive sight - 30 meters from the tip of his nose to the tip of his tail and scales the color of polished copper.

If you saw Zev streaking through the sky, you might think he was a dragon, but he wasn't a dragon. He was a native of the planet Scalaya. And even though the natives of the planet Scalaya are large, vaguely reptilian creatures with long necks, long tails and shining scales, they aren't dragons. They're actually not overly fond of being called dragons.

The atmosphere of Methes continued to thin under the beating of Zev's wings…

(The Scalayans also have large, bat-like wings. But, again, they're not dragons.)

...but it didn't matter. The Scalayans were first born in space, aeons ago, and moved from star to star for countless millennia before arriving on what eventually became their home planet back when it was still a young, evolving world. Zev reached out through his wings and felt not for the air, but for the gravitational fields of the world below and pushed off with such force that his speed began increasing geometrically. The pod stayed right behind him, held tight by the same manipulation of gravity that now moved him through the vacuum of space.

Zev craned his head back to the pod containing the Methens, an action which wasn't really necessary since he was projecting his thoughts into their minds.

"We have cleared the atmosphere and will soon be jumping into null space," his voice sounded softly and calmly into the minds of the three women and one man in the pod. "It won't take us much longer to reach..."

A silent shaft of energy interrupted his thoughts. It blasted close, too close to his left wing. He cursed under his breath and saw the outlines of the Stryker as it became visible. The small attack craft was streaking up from the planet below and had obviously been rendered invisible by a powerful spell - one Zev's ultra-vision couldn't see through.

Before the craft could retarget and fire again, Zev swung round - hurling the pod away from the planet while keeping his body between it and the Stryker. With a blinding speed the crew of the attack craft could barely follow, Zev closed the distance between them, saying a silent thanks that the crew didn't have better aim.

As he closed in on the craft, his massive jaws opened exposing a row of razor-sharp teeth and from deep within his throat a glow began to rise. A split second later a shaft of fiery light emerged from deep within his throat...

(I know what you're thinking - "But he's breathing fire." Well, yes, sort of, technically. The Scalayans have a pair of glands in the back of their throats that produce two different chemicals - things never heard of here on Earth - that when combined and exhaled produce a shaft of plasma energy that looks not totally unlike a flame. They hurl it from their mouths at tremendous velocity using the same gravitational manipulation they use to fly through space. But they really, really aren't dragons. And you really, really shouldn't call them dragons. They'll get… irritated.)

…and tore across the remaining distance and slammed into the Stryker.

The small craft was shielded, either magically or technologically - Zev couldn't tell - and survived the first onslaught. It did, however, break away from its pursuit of the pod and tried to put some distance between itself and Zev, whilst unsteadily trying to reposition itself to fire again. It quickly got to where it wanted to be and did what it wanted to do, but Zev wasn't entirely defenseless.

At the last second, he whirled around and let his back take the blast. He felt a searing pain as the heaviest section of his copper scales absorbed the blast. He felt them grow searingly hot and melt just slightly - it would take some time for them to heal - but he was otherwise unharmed. But he knew couldn't take another hit there and the scales over the rest of his body, his belly in particular, were not as strong.

Zev returned fire, hitting the Stryker again. It was a full on hit, but much further away than before and not as effective. Though he could see it took a toll on the craft's shields.

The Stryker was moving away again, this time arcing around Zev at a safe distance and closing in on the pod. Zev, redoubled his efforts and pushed as hard as he could against the nearby planet's gravity and closed in on the craft. Another plasma burst and he saw the shields were down, but the Stryker

3

was getting too close to the pod and Zev wasn't sure he could recharge his breath quickly enough.

With a last bit of extra effort, Zev gave a final push against the Methen gravity field and flung himself toward the craft. He got close enough to it to dig a powerful fore-claw into the metal of the hull. Then another. Then the claws of both rear legs. The craft was about half as long as Zev and when he grabbed it, the two started spinning staggeringly through the void - the Stryker's engines at full throttle and Zev trying to get a good hold on the constantly spinning gravitational field.

Zev finally bent his long neck down, opened his jaws again and sank his teeth into the hull of the craft, which yielded easily. If the crew wasn't taken by surprise by the sudden rending and tearing of the metal around the crew compartment, they probably would have been somewhat taken aback at the sudden loss of all atmosphere and pressure. Then, a mere second later, they would have been positively stunned as the cabin filled with superheated plasma.

But not for more than the fraction of a second it would have taken their bodies to disintegrate and the Stryker to explode.

Zev was ready for the impact of the explosion. It hurt, but did no further damage - though he was stunned for a second or two. When he came to his senses, instinct took over and he opened his jaws again and emitted what, had there been an atmosphere, would have been an ear-shattering roar. Though no one in space can hear you roar, since the Scalayans were actually born in space, over time they evolved the ability to send out what is essentially a roar on a range of energy frequencies - including radio frequencies. There was no one around that could detect the roar, but the blast that hit radio receivers across Methes definitely got some attention.

It would also be detected on many different worlds, but the speed of light being what it is, it would be some time before that happened.

In his mind, he could hear the worried and frantic shouts of the Methens inside the pod.

"Everything's okay," he said calmly. "A little trouble with some Zolanites, but it's taken care of." Zev moved, somewhat achingly toward the pod and felt his gravitational manipulation take hold. They started moving away from the planet again and Zev reached out ahead of them with his mind to open a hole in space for them to slip through.

"I'm opening a null space portal," Zev said. "Once we jump, it'll be just a couple of hours to Scalaya." Known space opened into completely unknown space and Zev and the pod dove in like it was a hotel swimming pool. "I think there is a pretty good supply of food and some whiskey in the pod, so why don't you all just sit back and enjoy the ride."

There was a clamor of thanks and gratitude from the minds of those in the pod and then even more thanks and gratitude when they discovered that it was actually really good whiskey.

First

What do you do when aliens kidnap your cat? I'll tell you what you don't do: You don't tell anyone. At best, you get laughed at or ridiculed. At worst, you still get laughed at and ridiculed, but you're in a straitjacket while they're doing it.

But, if you actually do tell someone and they don't take any of the preceding courses of action, don't listen to them if they say they know what to do. They probably don't. And it's even worse if they actually do know what to do. That just leads to more trouble. But more on that later. Back to the question at hand. What do you do when aliens kidnap your cat?

Let's start at the beginning.

The orange tabby cat lazily rolled over in a particularly sunny spot on the floor. He was slightly annoyed having to do this due to the fact the particular sunny spot he'd decided to occupy kept moving. There were plenty of other sunnier spots around the house, but this one was by far his favorite. It was fairly centrally located so he could keep track of everything going on around him. It also happened to be in the exact perfect place to be completely in the way of anyone wishing to go pretty much anywhere in the small house.

That gave him a number of opportunities. If he was feeling in a good mood, he could playfully paw at anyone who stepped over him. If he was in a bad mood, he could angrily paw at anyone who stepped over him. If he was in a totally indifferent mood, he could lazily paw at anyone who stepped over him.

If he was sleepy, he could stretch out and sleep in a way that was optimally inconvenient for anyone who stepped over him.

So far today, no one had tried to step over him and the spot was particularly warm and sunny.

It was a good day.

Mr. Sunshine was the name humans knew him by. As for what his name actually was, well, talk to T.S. Eliot about that. But, on a related note that will come up later, there is another name. An ancient name. Something no one, even Mr. Eliot, would have guessed.

Names aside, Mr. Sunshine came to live with Jack some three years ago. There was a girlfriend at the time and she'd seen the young, scraggly feline on the street and decided it needed a home over Jack's protest that the animal looked perfectly happy where it was. Once home, fed and curled up in an entirely different pool of sunlight, the girlfriend had named him Mr. Sunshine because he looked like "a little, cute puff of sunshine." Jack wasn't happy about any of it, but he agreed to let Mr. Sunshine stay because a cat is often a small price to pay for having an actual girlfriend.

Jack was, of course, annoyed to no end by Mr. Sunshine and Mr. Sunshine was very well aware of this and reveled in it. They had a daily routine of Jack doing the human things Jack did and Mr. Sunshine doing the cat things Mr. Sunshine did in the exact same spaces Jack was trying to do his particular activities.

After a time however, the two came to an understanding, even a reluctant respect for each other, which was a good thing because six months later the girlfriend was gone and three years later Mr. Sunshine was still stretched out napping on the floor of Jack's house.

While Mr. Sunshine was lounging, Jack sat nearby, deeply engrossed in a book.

At this point it should be noted that "Jack" is not Jack's real name. It's a name he decided to use for this story because "Jack" sounds much more "actiony" - his word - than his real name.

If you knew his real name, you'd agree.

Though he's loath to admit it, at no point in this story is Jack an "actiony" kind of guy. He tends to be on the bookish side of average and the boring side or ordinary. Up to this point, he'd lived most of his life within ten miles of where he grew up, except for the eight years he spent in college to get the advanced degrees necessary to get a job selling photocopy paper and, the year he spent in a city hours away actually trying to pursue a career related to the degrees. Obviously, it didn't work out. The career or the city.

So, he returned to his hometown, where there just happened to be a photocopy paper related job, which required his exact education and expertise, available. He tried for a while to make the photocopy paper business sound interesting. The problem is, it is so totally uninteresting that trying to make it sound interesting just makes you sound desperate and boring.

You might think this has nothing to do with the story other than random background information about Jack. You might even ask why this information and no description of the protagonist's steely blue eyes, his square jaw, his jet black hair and trim, muscled physique?

There are, in fact, two reasons: One, Jack has none of those physical qualities - rather, he has the opposite. His physical qualities are exactly what you'd imagine someone who would make a career involving photocopy paper would be. Secondly, it is exactly the reason Jack agreed to take in Mr. Sunshine.

When it came to romance in his life, selling photocopy paper wasn't the most enticing of lifestyles. Agreeing to adopt a kitten helped even out the balance sheet. On the rare occasions a woman does actually return to his house, they show definite pleasure at the fact Jack has a cat. Sadly, though, they usually end up liking the cat better.

Back to the events at hand, it was some moments later when Mr. Sunshine rolled again, stretched, yawned, and got up. He surveyed the room and saw the human sitting there reading a book. The sunshine was nice but he felt outside beckoning. He slowly walked over to the door, looking back at Jack. Jack didn't notice at first, so Mr. Sunshine meowed.

Jack stretched, yawned, got up and slowly walked over to the door and opened it allowing Mr. Sunshine access to the large back yard. The cat showed his appreciation by butting his head into Jack's shin and then made his way into the yard.

Jack returned to his book.

Most people learn there are five senses.

There is some argument for additional senses, such as the muscles' sense of which way is up, senses of hunger and thirst, sense of when the bladder or intestines are full. (I'm sure sense of style and sense of humor are in there as well.) So many people who make a fuss over this type of thing say there are really somewhere between 14 and 20 senses, none of which - apparently - have the same qualities as the so-called "sixth sense" - enhanced intuitiveness or awareness beyond normal perception. Something beyond what we consider a normal amount of our senses.

There may or may not be such a thing as a "sixth sense," or a "15th sense" or "21st sense" or anything in-between, in human beings. It could be that those incidents - which are chalked up to such a notion - are merely tricks of the brain decoding data collected by the other senses the sensor was unaware of. That would make it more a matter of processing data, or recognizing patterns, than sensing something that's not there.

Sometimes it might just be coincidence or just statistical probability when, say, someone phones up to tell you their grandmother was smashed by a semi while riding her Harley and you say "I had a feeling something bad had happened when you called." There's probably nothing supernatural about that. When you pick up the phone and hear your friend's sad voice, in the back of your mind you put all the clues together: his love for his grandmother, her penchant for motorcycles, the fact that cross-county biking may not be the best activity for a ninety-year-old. And just like déjà vu might be caused by a lag in time between you experiencing a moment and that moment registering in your brain, then a "sixth sense" (Would "nth sense" actually be more appropriate?) may simply be the cognitive wheels turning without one's knowledge.

Whatever the explanation, about fifteen minutes later Jack got a funny feeling and went to peek out the window to check on Mr. Sunshine. He saw the cat, sitting nonchalantly atop the patio table watching three aliens close in on him.

Second

*Y*ou'll have to forgive the interruption for just a second. I know the writer is trying to tell the story in the clearest way possible, but there really is a whole lot more to any story than just the bare facts. There's so much background to go into which, while it may not be something that needs to make it into print, it's very relevant to the story because it colors in the lines of who a person is and why they do what they do.

Who a person is, any person, is largely the sum of their experiences. Whether those experiences are positive or negative, and whether those experiences have a positive or negative effect, these are the things that shape each of us and make us who we are. Some things in our lives have more of an effect.

Let's talk about copy paper, for example. Not to spoil anything, but there are no photocopiers featured in this story. However, my graduate thesis was on the historic trends of fiber density in the seven different basic grades of copy paper. It took two years of research.

This does not impact the story at all, except that it was a very important two years in my life and shaped the person I am today, or at least who I was at this point in the story. That shaping is still here, I guess, but some other things kind of overwhelmed it.

I just want everyone to realize this, because actually reading about myself as the story is being written makes me sound rather… sad. Is this really how he sees me in this story?

The writer is glaring at me now. Sorry...

Here's the thing about aliens Jack didn't know at this particular point in his life: Aliens either look remarkably like ordinary humans or they look remarkably totally unlike ordinary humans. Believe it or not, the universe is populated with two-armed, two-legged, very human-looking bipeds whose only difference - if they look at all different - is bumpy foreheads or weird ears. Sometimes they have five fingers and toes. Sometimes they have three. Occasionally they have six, but never more than seven for some reason.

Then, there are those aliens that are really and truly "alien." They may be amorphous blobs, they may be floating bags of gas with tentacles or they may be somewhere between animals and plants or giant insect-like creatures. (We're talking intelligent races here. When you get into other things, it really gets weird out there.) There are also quite a few races of intelligent machines out there.

But the thing about it is, no matter what they look like, you recognize them instantly. Even the most human looking ones just seem... alien. And not like, oh, David Bowie always seemed like an alien or that guy who works in the accounting department is so weird he must be from another planet. You just kind of have to experience the alienness of aliens to understand.

The ones with tentacles though, you probably get that.

Seeing three beings of any type - human or not - closing in menacingly on his cat would have disturbed Jack. But seeing three... beings... (because though Jack didn't know they were aliens at this point, he knew there was something off about them) - closing in on Mr. Sunshine sent him into action.

Jack was not the most aggressive or assertive person. He wasn't particularly large or particularly small. He was average height, average build with average hair, eyes, nose, etc. (We've been through this already.) That is to say he was pretty ordinary and not exceptionally brave, though not necessarily a coward, or any more so than the average person would be in a given situation.

If he'd stopped to think about charging into a situation where three strangers were menacing his cat, he might have thought better of it and let Mr. Sunshine fend for himself. But, as it was, he was out the door and charging the trio before the thought "Hang on a second..." could even jump the gaps between his various neurons.

"What the hell are you doing in my yard!" Jack shouted as he leapt through the door and closed in on the trio.

They stared back at him and their strangeness started to seep in. That "This is a bad idea" train of thought finally made the right neuronic leap and Jack went from bold to "bad idea" in a matter of nanoseconds.

Mr. Sunshine turned casually and looked at him as well, as if he was wondering what all the commotion was about. He was uneasy about the three new creatures in his territory, but he felt his show of indifference to them would handle the situation. Now his creature had entered the situation and, somehow, he felt it wouldn't make things better.

None of the three spoke as Jack accosted them. They simply glanced at one another and then looked back at Jack as he approached. Jack was trying to look intimidating, but it wasn't really working out for him.

One of the three made a noise that, upon reflection Jack decided was speech, because one of the others replied with similar noises. They seemed unconcerned and started moving forward toward Mr. Sunshine again, basically ignoring Jack.

Both Jack and the alien trio reached the patio table at the same time. Jack reached out and took Mr. Sunshine up in his arms and started to back away. Mr. Sunshine was annoyed at being scooped up against his will and switched to disgruntled indifference.

"I don't know what you guys are doing here, but I'm calling the…"

There might have been more to that sentence - possibly the word "police" - but any potential additional information, threats or, indeed, intelligible words were halted by two things: The first was the small object at the back of his yard that looked suspiciously like what one would think a small spaceship would look like. The second was that one of the aliens took a small rod out from somewhere inside his clothing and pointed it at Jack.

Jack didn't know what the object was, but he knew his best course of action was to not stick around to find out. He turned and dashed toward the still open door. Fortunately for him, he stumbled after about two steps and went down, sending an indignant Mr. Sunshine flying off to his left. The fortunate part is that just as he fell, something whizzed over his head and slammed into the open door with an impact that caused it to splinter.

In an instant, Jack saw this, then looked to see that Mr. Sunshine was running to safety away from the trio. He tried to go somewhere much safer in a completely different direction, but wasn't entirely sure what direction that might be. All three of the strangers had similar somethings in their hands. Two others pointed at him and suddenly energy bolts were zipping past him and punching holes in the rear wall of his kitchen.

He scrambled again, looking for cover. As he did, bolts stuck around him. Some struck the back of the house, further splintering the walls and roof. Others did in his lawn furniture. After about fifteen seconds of an intense barrage, Jack found two of the three had closed in on him and the third was approaching Mr. Sunshine, who was backed up under a bush by the fence.

"What the hell is going on here?" Jack said pleadingly at the two approaching him.

One of them made another series of strange noises and pointed the device in his hand at him, which Jack realized looked remarkably like a wand.

There was a spark and then blackness.

Jack had never been unceremoniously rendered unconscious by anything other than boring lectures, boring movies or rather exciting drinks. When he came to some undetermined time later, if he'd known the exact method used to render him unconscious, he probably would have fainted away. And in this instance his headache would have been secondary to wonder and disbelief of realizing he had been knocked out by a jolt of magic from a wand.

But, he didn't know this and, honestly, it probably wouldn't have toned down the throbbing in his head because it hurt quite a bit.

"Here. Drink this," a voice he didn't immediately recognize said.

A rather blurry person placed an equally blurry object that felt like a bowl in his hand. The bowl contained water, which it goes without saying was also quite a bit blurry. He was curious why it was in a bowl, but his head hurt too much to go any further with that line of thinking at the moment. He raised the bowl to his lips and drank. The water was room temperature and not too pleasant. It also had something in it that may or may not have been cat fur.

After a second, he spat it out.

"This is the cat's water bowl!" He said dropping it on the floor and splashing the water.

"Sorry," said the figure. "It was the only water I saw."

Jack got up spitting cat hair and staggered across the room to the sink. He was in his kitchen now. He got to where the sink

15

had been and realized it was gone, or rather it had been blasted into pieces along with most of the rest of the room. Jack's vision was clearing up a bit and he noticed just how wrecked the kitchen was.

"You could have just gotten it from the bathroom faucet," he said, stumbling over the debris in the general direction of the bathroom.

"I didn't know where it was," the slightly less blurry figure said. "I got you dragged in here and gave you the first water I found."

Jack mumbled something, ducked into the hallway bathroom, ran a lot of water for several minutes then came back out with a wet towel on his head.

"What the hell happened?" He said looking around. Then it hit him.

"Mr. Sunshine!" He started running for where the door used to be, but the figure moved in front of him. He got a much less blurry look at the figure and instantly recognized it.

"If you're looking for the cat, they took it," the other said. "Don't know why. Odd move for aliens. Never knew 'em to take cats before."

Jack just stared at the man for a few seconds. What he'd said didn't really sink in.

"I know you," Jack finally said. "You're UFO Bob."

The other man just looked at him, deadpan.

"Yeah," he said. "Or, just Bob. Without the 'UFO' part. That works too. But that's me."

"What are you doing here? And what do you mean they took Mr Sunshine?"

"Well, I mean they took your cat, who I guess is named Mr. Sunshine. Weird name for a cat," he rubbed the stubble on his chin. "They've been gone about five minutes."

Jack stumbled into the back yard and looked around at the destruction there. He noticed a large burned area in the back and saw the fence had taken quite a beating as well.

"But why are you here?" Jack finally turned and faced UFO Bob. "And did you say aliens? Surely you didn't say aliens did you?"

"Yup, I said aliens," he said, stepping out into the yard as well. "Saw their ship and followed it. Been seeing them around for a couple of weeks now. Knew they were looking for something. Didn't think it was a cat though."

Jack's head started spinning from something other than the headache. He looked for someplace to sit. He looked around and noticed there wasn't a chair. At least not one in any condition to be sat upon. So he plopped down on the debris-strewn kitchen floor, the wet towel still draped over his head.

"What's going on here? Am I going crazy?" Jack slumped, propping his head in his hands. He sat there for a moment, then looked up. UFO Bob was just standing there looking down at him.

"Why would you be going crazy?" He asked with all sincerity.

Jack just stared at him.

"Seriously?" He said, climbing to his feet then motioning around. "I'm standing here in the ruins of my kitchen being told by someone I barely know that aliens, actual aliens from outer space, just kidnapped my cat."

He took in a large breath.

"That just might cause one to lose one's grip on reality."

UFO Bob shrugged.

"I guess."

UFO Bob walked toward the back yard. Reluctantly Jack followed.

"The thing to do now is figure out why they kidnapped a cat," UFO Bob said walking around the burned spot where the alien craft was sitting a few minutes earlier.

"That's odd behavior. Even for aliens."

"Wait a minute," Jack said, stopping in the wreckage of his yard. "How exactly do you know they were really aliens?"

"You mean aside from them climbing into their spaceship and taking off?"

Jack shook his head.

"Maybe they were some kind of secret government operatives on some covert mission using some kind of advanced technology…"

"To come and take your cat," UFO Bob said flatly. "You seriously think government agents came and took your cat?

"People say I'm the one who's crazy," UFO Bob muttered.

"Well, it makes as much sense as aliens," Jack retorted. "Besides, they didn't look very alien."

"Some of them don't," Bob said. "But a lot of them… Well, they look very alien."

"Oh?" Jack said indignantly. He was getting tired of this nonsense and tired of UFO Bob's crazy stories. "I suppose you've seen a lot of aliens, have you?"

UFO Bob shook his head.

"No," he said. "Counting these three only about half a dozen different species. In real life, that is. I've seen sketches and photos of several more."

Jack stared at UFO Bob for a second, then threw up his hands in frustration.

"Fine. Whatever." Jack said, surrendering to the insanity.

"I've got to find someone to tell what happened. Or at least to tell a plausible story about what happened without all your alien nonsense."

Jack turned away from UFO Bob and started around his house.

"How am I going to explain this to the insurance company?" he grumbled.

"I guess I'll have to drive into town and let…"

He stopped as he rounded the corner of his house and saw the pile of scrap metal that used to be a car.

"Shit…" was all he managed a moment after realizing what he was looking at.

"Oh yeah," UFO Bob said, walking up next to him. "They did that before they left. I think they thought it was another spaceship and they blew it up to keep anyone from following them. Though, I couldn't make out exactly what they were saying. They were speaking a dialect I didn't really understand too well."

Jack turned and looked at UFO Bob, let out a sigh and started walking. He realized the damp towel was still draped over his head and slid it off onto his shoulder.

"I guess I'll walk then," he said. "Maybe the police won't lock me up right away for telling crazy stories. They can at least see all of…" he stopped and gestured toward the house and car, "…this."

"I really wouldn't tell anyone," UFO Bob said, catching up to Jack as he headed down the road toward town. "They might think you're nuts."

"That's really great advice coming from you," Jack snapped. "You're the one who just said this whole thing didn't sound crazy."

"Well yeah," UFO Bob said. "From my point of view it isn't."

Jack wanted to scream, instead he just plodded down the road toward town. UFO Bob fell into step beside him.

Third

In general, Jack liked where he lived. It was a couple of miles from town, but still isolated. You had to be very deliberate in coming to his home. It wasn't a place where people could stop and say "I was just passing by..."

The road leading to his house was lined on each side by woods, a few fields, an old barn - an occasional cow or two. (It's actually pretty interesting: though it wasn't generally known, the cows actually were only cows occasionally. Most people weren't quite sure what they were at other times, but one person knew. And he knew just how dangerous the truth would be if it ever got out.) But otherwise the road and the land leading to Jack's house was largely unremarkable and relatively rural.

About fifteen minutes into their walk, they came to a bridge crossing a small creek. It was an ordinary bridge crossing an ordinary creek. Jack had crossed it a million times. Actually, Jack had crossed that bridge 7,927 times in his lifetime and in all those times there had never been a strange woman standing right in the middle of the bridge.

Jack didn't have time to realize he didn't recognize her because in the time it would have normally taken to realize this, his brain was too astounded by the realization that this woman was an alien. It was instantly followed by the thought that such a thing was nonsense and just more of UFO Bob's rantings creeping into his brain. But then, there was also part of his brain screaming "THIS WOMAN IS AN ALIEN!"

Jack stopped, clutching the ends of the towel draped around his shoulder, his mind still trying to come to grips with all the conflicting thoughts racing through his brain. He looked at UFO Bob, who had a big grin on his face. Bob raised a hand and made a complicated gesture with his fingers and said something that sounded not entirely like some of the noises the other people... government agents... aliens who couldn't possibly be aliens because... whatever... made when Jack saw them in his yard.

The woman stared at UFO Bob, obviously slightly confused and wary.

"It's okay," UFO Bob whispered to Jack. "I just gave a universal greeting." He paused and looked thoughtful for a second. "I think I did anyway."

The woman finally raised her hand, made a similar sign and spoke a similar phrase. UFO Bob showed obvious relief. She then pointed at them both and indicated they should follow her into the nearby woods. UFO Bob started after her immediately, but saw Jack wasn't moving.

The last half an hour or so had already been trying for Jack and the idea of going off into the woods with a strange woman - who might actually be an alien - they just met randomly on a country road didn't seem like the best idea. It never turned out well in the movies.

"Don't worry," UFO Bob said. "It worked." He grabbed Jack's arm and started moving slowly following the woman.

"I'm pretty sure she's not going to eat us," Bob said giving Jack a grin.

"Oh, great," Jack said without much enthusiasm. "I feel much better now."

They were silent as they followed the woman into the woods. In spite of her "alienness" Jack noticed she was actually very human looking. Pleasantly human looking in fact.

Maybe a little more orange than usual in the way of a spray tan gone wrong, but not in a displeasing way.

UFO Bob finally broke the silence.

"That's actually the first time I've ever done that," he said softly, but with obvious pleasure and excitement in his voice.

"And just how did you know to do that?" Jack asked, finally just surrendering a bit to the absurdity of it all. "I suppose you were kidnapped by aliens and learned to speak to them."

"I was taken by aliens a couple of times," UFO Bob said. "Though 'kidnapped' is a strong word. Once I realized who they were, I was happy to go."

"Okay, fine," Jack said taking a breath. "And that's how you learned to speak to them?"

"No," UFO Bob said. "I found some videos online."

"Of course you did…"

They went about half a mile, by Jack's poor reckoning, through the woods and into a clearing beyond. The rest of the journey was made in silence, with the woman glancing back every now and again to make sure the pair was following. Part of Jack's brain was still wondering why, exactly, he and a guy he hardly knew were following a strange woman they just met randomly on the road - after he'd been attacked, his cat kidnapped and his home destroyed - into the deep, remote woods, where most likely no one would hear you scream - if in fact screaming became a factor in this venture.

It seemed more and more that maybe this wasn't the smartest action.

But most of his brain was still reeling from the idea of aliens, from the destruction of his home and car and kidnapping of his cat, and from the blast he took from what looked like a magic wand wielded by the trio that attacked him.

Since his brain couldn't agree on exactly what to do or what was going on, it figured the best thing to do right now was simply to do nothing and go with the flow, taking the rest of Jack - somewhat unwillingly - along with it.

Unfortunately, going with the flow was not always Jack's strongest suit. The flow made him nervous. Visibly jittery. He much preferred watching the flow from a distance. Or better yet, being somewhere far away from the flow. Reading a book. With his cat.

Mr. Sunshine... Jack thought painfully. He realized he missed the cat more than he liked to admit. To him, cats represented stability. When you had a cat, your cat was like the foundation of your home - your place to be. Dogs were good. Jack liked dogs. But dogs wandered and if you wandered with your dog, everywhere you went was just as good as everywhere else - exciting, new. No matter how many times you'd been there.

Cats established a fixed point in the universe that was theirs. They were like cosmic "You Are Here" signs. When you had a cat in your home, it was your HOME. Your place. Or at least the place they let you share with them that was their HOME.

Jack wanted his HOME back desperately.

Eventually, they stepped into a clearing and Jack stopped abruptly while his brain tried to decide on which insane thing to focus on first - as there were several to choose from. It took only nanoseconds, but his brain finally prioritized the insanity in order from least to most insane.

First on the list was someone who was, again, obviously alien even though they looked completely human. Just a hint of bad spray-on tan. This in itself wasn't the insane part, since they'd been following a woman who fit that category as well for a while now. The insane part was how he was dressed. He wore long flowing robes covered in what looked like stars, moons and galaxies and had a tall, pointy hat to match. Jack's first thought was he looked like an escapee from The Sorcerer's Apprentice.

The second insane thing was the silver bubble floating a few feet off the ground. There was an opening in the side with a ladder coming down to the ground. Obviously a spaceship, but a little disappointing. It didn't look very science fiction.

Third, and this was the BIG one - literally - was… Jack blinked. Was…

"Holy shit! It's a dragon!"

The woman spun round at the sound of his raised voice. The other alien looked startled as well. Even UFO Bob's mouth hung open.

The creature, who was easily 20 meters long from head to tail and covered in blue-green scales, raised its head slowly toward the new arrivals. It made a growling deep in its throat, then looked to the woman. She stepped toward Jack and UFO Bob and started speaking rather excitedly, not looking at all happy.

There was another growl from the creature and the woman turned back toward it and nodded slightly, then stepped away toward the other alien. The larger creature then stood on its hind legs and took a step toward Jack and UFO Bob. Its eyes glistened.

Jack griped his towel in fear.

"Forgive me for startling you," came a voice from nowhere. Jack couldn't find the source, then realized it was actually inside his head.

"Yes, Jack," the voice said. *"I'm speaking to both you and Bob telepathically so you can understand what I'm saying. With your permission, I will alter your brain chemistry just slightly - it will do no damage so no need to be alarmed - to enable you both to understand our languages."*

"Absolutely!" UFO Bob burst out enthusiastically. "Please do!"

Jack wasn't so sure. When it came to giant dragons digging around in his brain after being lured into the woods by an alien woman whilst on his way to report his house had been destroyed and his cat kidnapped by different aliens, he was somewhat apprehensive.

"I promise, Jack," the voice said. *"It will do no harm. Afterwards you will feel nothing different."*

"Well..." Jack started. "I suppose..."

"There," the creature growled and Jack understood what it was saying. "It is done."

"Amazing!" UFO Bob gushed. "I understood you!"

"Good," the woman said, striding over to the pair of them, obviously angry. "Then you'll understand me when I throttle which ever one of you let those bastards take that cat."

Jack was taken aback at her ferocity. He took a slight step backwards.

"I didn't exactly 'let' them take Mr. Sunshine," he finally stammered, trying to defend himself. "They didn't give me much choice."

"Mr. Sunshine," the woman smirked. "That's a stupid name for a cat."

Jack opened his mouth to respond. He was going to explain how the name came about. How it wasn't him but his then girlfriend and how, when you have a girlfriend and she wants to name a cat Mr. Sunshine, you just go with it, but the creature spoke first.

"Calm down Jal," it said in a soft growl. "We couldn't possibly expect these humans to defend themselves against the Zolanites. There's no need to be angry with them."

Jack smiled weakly.

"Exactly," he said quickly. "I confronted them and they started shooting me with their ray guns. They blew up my house and knocked me unconscious and took Mr. Sunshine. It's like the nice dragon said, I couldn't…"

Jack was interrupted by a growl from above that, while not exactly interpreted was definitely understood as displeasure. The woman stepped up to Jack and grabbed his shirt.

"Don't call them that!" she said angrily. "It's not very nice!"

Jack was stunned.

"Don't call them what?" He was confused. "You mean drag…ACK!"

The grip on his shirt tightened.

"I understand," he finally gasped. "I won't use the 'D' word."

"Jal," the creature finally said. "It's okay. He doesn't understand. He meant no harm."

Jal let go of Jack and took a deep breath.

"I'm sorry," she finally said. "But that word is considered insulting to the Scalayans," she turned and nodded to the creature. "That's her race. The Scalayans. My people - we're Methens by the way - owe the Scalayans everything.

"I get a little… defensive… at times."

Jal stepped back away from Jack.

"Really? I hadn't noticed."

"It's quite all right," UFO Bob said, laughing nervously and stepping between Jal and Jack. "There's always bound to be some slight misunderstandings when meeting new species."

He patted them both slightly on their shoulders, still nervously tittering.

"Well said," the other alien said stepping forward. "And I wish there was time to stand here and explain things, but now that we know the Zolanites have the cat, we need to get back and let Barry and the others know."

"Indeed," the Scalayan said. "They're well on their way back to Methes now. We must make plans before Zola has a chance to strike."

Jack was looking between all three and growing more and more confused.

"Wait," he said. "What?"

And then.

"Who's Barry?"

"Don't worry human Jack," the Scalayan said. "There's no need to worry further. I've looked into your mind. There's nothing you could have done to stop the Zolanites and you have no other information that would be of use to us."

"You've looked into..."

"We'll leave you now," the Scalayan said.

"But, what about Mr. Sunshine?"

"If we can, we will save him from Zola and return him to you," the Scalayan said. "If not... Well, then it is doom for us all."

All three looked very somber at the mention of this. Well, two of them at least. Jack wasn't very good at reading the expressions on the face of drag.... Scalayans...

"Doom?" was all Jack came up with. He really wasn't following a lot of what was going on, but he was beginning to get the gist of it, and it wasn't a good thing. He didn't want to get the gist of it because he was pretty sure that would lead to even more things he absolutely didn't want to know about.

There was silence, followed by not silence.

"We want to come with you!" An obviously excited UFO Bob exclaimed, breaking the darkening mood.

"You've got to be kidding," Jal said.

"Wait," Jack said after a pause. "What?"

"Yes!" UFO Bob stepped toward the Scalayan. "We definitely want to come with you. I don't know exactly what's going on, but it sounds important. It also sounds like it will affect us. But it will definitely affect Jack's cat and Jack really wants his cat back. So we want to be part of whatever this is."

Jal looked at her two companions. The other Methen shrugged. Jal turned back and eyed Jack and UFO Bob.

"I don't know…"

"They have good intentions," the Scalayan said. "We need all the allies we can get.

"Besides, I sense there's more to them both than we can see or that even they are aware of. I think we should let them come."

"Yes! Please." UFO Bob said. His face lit up like a kid eying a free trip to the candy store.

"Wait," Jack said more insistently. "What?"

Jal rubbed her chin, obviously thinking it over. Finally, she came to a decision.

"Very well," she said. "You're welcome to come and join us in our fight against the evil witch Zola and her minions.

"But we have to hurry. Climb on board and I'll fill you in on everything you need to know on the way back to Scalaya."

UFO Bob gleefully grabbed Jack by the arm and started dragging him to the ship. The man in the hat and robes was already climbing in and the woman, Jal, waited for the rest to get up the ladder. She looked at Jack as he passed.

"Is that a towel?" She asked as she pulled it from Jack's shoulders.

"Um, yeah," Jack said, remembering he'd brought it with him. "I wet it down after I'd been zapped by those three… um, guys…"

Jal took the towel and tossed it aside.

"It's fine," she said. "You won't need a towel."

She prodded him up the ladder and Jack heard UFO Bob just ahead snickering.

"Wait," he said. "What?"

28

Fourth

Jal explained things.

"My name is Jal," Jal said after getting everyone situated in the surprisingly comfortable craft. Jack looked around and saw nothing that looked like controls. Only seating and what looked like some sort of supply cabinet off to one side.

"This," she indicated the other Methen, "is my baby brother Orlo."

"Younger brother," Orlo said, giving a little wave to Jack and UFO Bob.

Jack noticed Orlo was definitely younger, definitely Jal's brother and definitely as alien feeling but as normal looking - aside from the over-the-top outfit - as Jal.

"And our companion is T'Ki. As I said before, she's from the planet Scalaya - where we're headed. My brother and I were both born on the planet Methes, which is ruled by the evil sorceress Zola, but we have been living on Scalaya for many years."

"She's not coming in? T'ki? How's she going to travel to another planet?" Jack asked, looking around and trying to figure out how a 20 meter long drag... Scalayan... would fit into the ship.

Then something else hit him.

"Wait. Did you say 'sorceress'?"

The two non-humans seemed to ignore the question.

"T'Ki will be guiding the transport back to Scalaya," Orlo said. "Scalayans are able to travel through space and open up portals to null space. They have the ability to manipulate gravitational forces which will let T'Ki carry the capsule along with her."

"I see," Jack said. He didn't, but decided it didn't matter.

"Anyway," Jack continued, "my name is Jack and this is UFO Bob."

UFO Bob grimaced.

"Or, just Bob," he said. "No UFO. I'm really excited about meeting you guys. I mean I've met some extraterrestrials from when they've taken me before and I've seen others in videos, but you're the first Methens…"

"I guess you can tell UFO Bob is a really big fan," Jack said. "Now, I believe you were explaining to us just what the hell is going on, what this 'doom' is you were talking about and just why, exactly, my cat is involved. And maybe mention why you said 'sorceress'?"

"This may be a bit strange to you," Orlo said, looking at Jal.

"Buddy," Jack said. He was finally getting his footing, but fully aware it might be jerked right out from under him and any moment. "We're light years beyond strange right now."

"This is the part where I go into lengthy exposition," Jal said. "But just hold off on any questions until I finish."

"Sure," UFO Bob agreed, obviously hanging onto her every word. Jack nodded. He already had so many questions, asking them would be pointless.

"First, a little history.

"Thousands of years ago, your years, Xanthol raiders visited your world and brought back some Earthers. As it turns out, two of that number were very powerful sorcerers, at least on your world. Out in the cosmos, not so much. They were brought to our home world, Methes, which was ruled by the Xanthians at the time.

"What they didn't realize was the red star Methes orbits slowly caused Zola, one of the sorcerers, to dramatically increase her powers. Eventually, she became powerful enough to overthrow the Xanthians and seize control of Methes for herself.

"In the chaos of her overthrow, however, a number of Methens managed to flee and wandered through space for years, including the other Earth sorcerer who we call Barry. His powers weren't enhanced by exposure to the red star.

"After a time, the fleeing Methens, along with Barry, were found by some Scalayans, including T'Ki…"

"Wait," Jack interrupted. "You're saying T'ki and this Zola are thousands of years old?"

Jal glared.

"Yes!" she hissed. "I said wait on your questions. You're disrupting the exposition."

Speaking of disrupting the exposition, I just feel like I have to mention something here. You might be thinking I should explain how magic is real or spaceships, aliens or cat-nappers are real, but I'm not. I'm going to tell you how weirdness works.

You'd think if something like your cat being kidnapped by aliens happened to you, followed by everything which has been chronicled up to this point, it might be just a tad overwhelming. But there is something interesting about the relation of weirdness to normalcy - if there is such a thing - or at least perceived normalcy. As weirdness increases, what seems - or what you accept as normal - increases as well. Slowly at first in relation to the weirdness, but then they reach a point of convergence where no matter how weird things get, they seem normal. Or even sub normal. Mundane in fact.

Here. I drew a graph that illustrates what I mean:

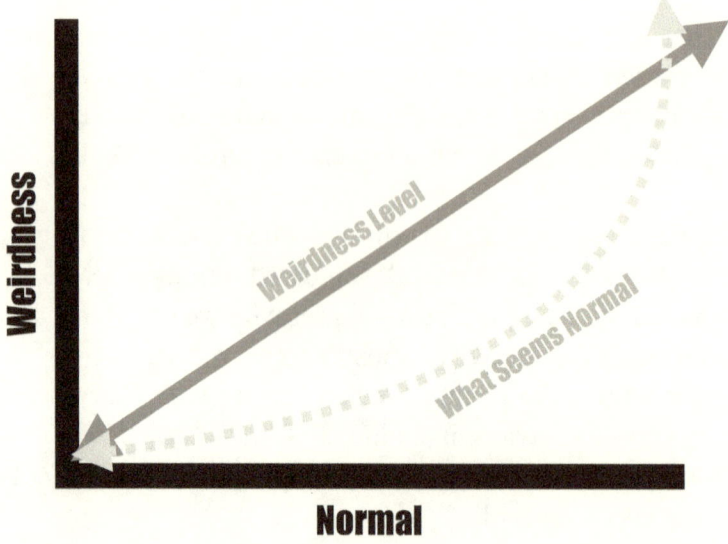

By the way, this graph was drawn on a sheet of 8 1/2 x 11, standard 20#, 100gsm long grain uncoated white. Just thought you might want to know that.

Back to the story…

"Anyway, as I was saying. The surviving Methens and Barry, who is also thousands of your years old, were taken back to Scalaya and offered a home there. Though they were happy to be free, they still longed for freedom for their fellow Methens and eventually began making plans with the Scalayans to try and oppose Zola and to rescue as many people from Methes as possible.

"Meanwhile, as years went on, Barry began to discover that the blue sun Scalaya orbits increased his powers just as the red one did for Zola. However, she had many more centuries under the red star and was and still is much more powerful than Barry, formidable as he is."

"So what exactly does Mr. Sunshine have to do with any of this?" Jack interrupted again, getting another glare from Jal and a punch in the arm from UFO Bob.

"I was getting to that," Jal said through gritted teeth.

"Sorry," he said.

"As I said, back on Earth, around five thousand of your years ago, Zola was a powerful witch. And as do many sorcerers, she had a familiar - a cat - named Utu Lu..."

"And you're saying Mr. Sunshine is this witch Zola's familiar?" Jack said, laying on the sarcasm.

"No. Not at all," Orlo said before Jal could say something even more insulting and possibly profane. "Cats don't live thousands of years. Their lives can't be magically extended like Barry's or Zola's. Utu Lu has been dead thousands of years."

Jack suddenly realized he was relieved to know the cat he'd shared his home with for so long wasn't the co-conspirator of a five-thousand year old evil space witch. Though, if that had been the case, it would explain a lot of Mr. Sunshine's behavior.

Jack even more suddenly realized just how weird the prior realization sounded in his head and it worried him that he wasn't worried about the weirdness. He pinched himself to see if it would wake him up from this increasingly bizarre dream. Jal and Orlo had puzzled looks as he pinched his arm and swore quietly at the pain. UFO Bob just smiled at him.

"Do go on," UFO Bob said to Jal.

"Obviously your cat couldn't be five thousand years old," she said condescendingly. "But, Zola is convinced your cat is one of the nine reincarnations of Utu Lu - the seventh, I believe - and if he is, which we are convinced of as well, and if she can reawaken his memories of that previous life in him, she will become even more powerful."

Jack opened his mouth to speak, but closed it when Jal narrowed her eyes.

"If that happens, not even the combined forces of the Methens, Scalayans and Barry would be able to oppose her. She could destroy us all."

33

Jal and Orlo looked gravely at Jack and UFO Bob. There was a long silence until it was interrupted by a soft "Wow" from UFO Bob.

Jack shook his head.

"Okay. That story is insane, but that's fine," he closed his eyes slowly and opened them hoping his surroundings would dissolve back to his nice, comfy home. They stubbornly refused to do so.

"I'm sorry to hear about this fight with this witch and the enslavement of your world and all, but I don't see how we can help. I just want to get my cat back and go home and forget about all of this."

"This is too big to forget about, Jack," UFO Bob said. "These people need our help."

"Yeah, right," Jack scowled. "I'm a photocopy paper salesman and you're a crackpot who believes aliens built the pyramids."

"Hey!" UFO Bob protested.

"No," Orlo said. "Your people built the pyramids. They just used alien technology.

"And magic, of course."

Jack slumped back in his seat.

"Fine," he moaned. "I'm beginning to think this was a bad idea…"

The journey to Scalaya took just over an hour. Jack mostly sat silently after the history lesson from Jal as UFO Bob chatted excitedly with the others. He only half listened as he seriously tried to make everything fit into his worldview that had suddenly been turned upside down. Less than two hours ago, things were normal. As far as he knew there were no ancient sorcerers, aliens, re-incarnated cats or other aliens who - and he honestly couldn't help himself here - really looked like dragons. (*I probably would have felt better at the time if I'd seen the graph I came up with.*)

Don't feel so bad Jack.

Jack jumped, startled by the sudden voice in his head before realizing it was T'ki speaking to him.

Sorry. I didn't mean to startle you again, her voice was soft and soothing.

There's a lot to get used to, Jack thought back, hoping this was how it worked. T'ki gave him reassurance she could understand him. *And talking with a giant creature flying through space using my mind isn't even on the top of the list.*

This brought about what could only have been a laugh from the Scalayan.

I sense how you're feeling, T'ki said. *And I know this isn't a path of your choosing, but if it helps, I think this is the path you were meant to be on. That you need to be on.*

Jack let out a long, physical sigh.

And what does that say about my life?

It says you have a life you value. And you value the lives of others - your cat included. And it says that there's something you haven't realized yet about yourself, but you have an inkling that it's there nonetheless. Maybe all of this will help you discover it.

If we survive, Jack replied.

There's always that, T'ki said. *But I have a good feeling about all of this.*

For now, just relax and rest. You've had a trying day.

Jack felt a little tension ease and wondered if he was actually feeling better or if T'Ki was somehow manipulating his brain again. Either way, he decided to go with it and leaned back, trying his best to embrace the calm he felt.

About halfway into the trip, Jal gave him a drink which she said would relax him a bit. It was tasty and highly alcoholic - probably some proof he was better off not telling his liver about. By the end of the trip, he was somewhat more relaxed. But as his mind drifted, then events of the past hour or so came rushing back rendering the amount of relaxation purely academic. Slowly his went from relaxed, to panicked to downright grumpy.

Jack was still in this mood when they landed and set foot on Scalaya, but as soon as he descended the ladder and looked up from the landing pad, everything - his mood, the stories he'd been told, the kidnapping of Mr. Sunshine, the destruction of his house - all melted away and he stood there by the little group and the ship and tried to comprehend the beauty and wonder of what he was seeing.

Simply put, Scalaya was the most beautiful place he'd ever seen.

The first thing he noticed was the city surrounding the landing pad - if you could call it a city. Jack actually couldn't decide if it was a city or a forest. Every structure looked as if it grew organically from the ground. There were things that were obviously trees. Tall, slender things with branches spreading out and intertwining to form canopies above the streets. Covered in leaves ranging the spectrum from greens to reds to brilliant oranges to brown.

Dwarfing the city were giant towers which appeared to be natural rock formations. Not mountains, but stone spires reaching hundred of feet into the sky. He saw openings in the spires, which he soon realized must be entrances to the abodes for the Scalayans.

But if the ground and the spires were awe-inspiring, the actual sky was something that just might fry your brain. The sun was either setting or rising. Jack couldn't tell. He just knew it was brilliant and blue and low on the horizon. But whatever time of day it was, the sky was like a dream. The sun was like a glowing sapphire in a sky that went from jade green to a deep, deep blue. But what made it even more spectacular was the sky was filled with Scalayans. They shone like multi-colored jewels in the sky, flying from spire to spire.

Jack stood, not moving, his mouth hanging open.

"It's... It's so beautiful..." he finally gasped. "It's like nothing..." was all he could add.

Jal and Orlo gave him a moment, but then Jal started getting impatient.

"We really need to be..."

"Hey!" UFO Bob almost shouted, startling Jack out of his state of wonder. "I think I've been here before."

T'Ki told the group she'd see them again after their meeting and took to the air. Jal and Orlo herded Jack and UFO Bob toward a low cluster of building-tree thingies at the base of the nearest spire. UFO Bob was chattering on about remembering a previous visit. Orlo was nodding patiently, but Jack was getting annoyed despite the beauty surrounding them.

"How could you have possibly been here before?" he said crossly.

"One of the times I was taken by aliens," UFO Bob chirped. "I think we might have come here. Some of this looks familiar. Maybe they masked my memories and seeing it now is jogging them back into place."

Jack just stared at UFO Bob then looked to Jal, who simply shrugged her shoulders.

"It's possible," she simply said and turned away and led them on.

Jack walked on in silence. This was by far the most amazing experience not just of his lifetime, but of anyone's life time and all he could think about was how much he really didn't want to be there. It might be fine for UFO Bob, but it was increasingly uncomfortable for him and that made him edgy and grouchy.

But then, the view...

He looked up at the sky again. The sun was definitely setting because it was disappearing over the horizon, but a soft light began to illuminate the city and the spires. The Scalayans still flew about overhead in complex, mesmerizing patterns. He felt his mood soften a bit. His grouchiness faded, but the edginess was still there.

"Where are we going?" he finally asked Jal.

"We're going to meet with the leadership council and fill them in on what happened," she said grimly. "Your cat's abduction may cause us to accelerate our plans."

"And just what does that mean?" Jack asked, not really wanting to know the answer he already knew.

"War."

"This day isn't exactly turning out the way I'd planned it," Jack said glumly.

Fifth

The trio of aliens were not happy.

Even to Methens, who'd never seen a cat, it was obvious that the hissing ball of fur they were carrying was epically upset.

He'd first shown his displeasure when one of the three aliens, Sala, grabbed him after shredding Jack's backyard. The alien was rewarded with numerous large scratches on his hands and arms. A second alien, Me'el, had the good sense to try and corral him into a small cage, but Mr. Sunshine was having none of that either.

It was the third alien, Tenga - who looked much less alien than his companions, but that doesn't play into the story just yet - who actually managed to lull Mr. Sunshine into a calm enough state to get him into the cage. He produced a small talisman and waved it in front of the bushes where Mr. Sunshine was hiding. After a few seconds, the growling and hissing stopped, the bush rustled and the dazed tabby stumbled out into the open. Tenga scooped him up and placed him in the cage.

By the time the trio made it back to Methes with the cage, Mr. Sunshine had emerged from his stupor and was once again expressing his displeasure. But, safely incarcerated, none of his captors paid him much mind. They carried the cage from their ship across a wide courtyard and into a large metallic and crystal pyramid towering over a cityscape of low buildings.

Once inside the pyramid, they made their way into a large chamber where a solitary figure sat. Sala and Me'el stayed near the entrance, but Tenga, carrying the cage, strode up to the figure sitting on a raised dais with her eyes closed.

"I have him, mother," he said, setting the cage on a dais before the woman. (This is where the not-as-alien-looking thing comes in, though if you were from a world other than Earth or Methes - where they currently were - he would still be completely alien. Not completely alien looking is a better description. Just like the whole deal with calling Scalayans the "D" word, sometimes referring to someone as "alien" is a definite faux pas.)

Zola slowly opened her eyes. Her gaze moved slowly from her son to the cage on the floor. A slight smile crossed her face.

"Were there any problems this time?"

"No mother," he said. "We made it there before the Scalayans. There was a human who tried to stop us, but we disposed of him."

"Did you now," she said suspiciously as she rose and stepped down to examine the cage more closely. "You're certain of that?"

Tenga looked hesitantly at his mother.

"Yes…" he started. "He was struck point blank by my own…"

"You might be interested to know that the Scalayan group has just returned with two humans. Both picked up in the area where you retrieved Utu Lu. That can't be a coincidence."

"Does that really matter?" Tenga snapped.

"No," she said, lifting the cage to get a better look at the growling Mr. Sunshine. "But it is another mistake in a series of problems that have arisen since I tasked you with this mission.

"I guess I expect too much from you. Your blood isn't pure after all. It's tainted. It seems that has weakened your powers more than I expected."

Tenga fumed in silence at his mother's words.

Zola looked into the cage. Her eyes fixed on the growling Mr. Sunshine.

"Yes..." she whispered. "I feel you in there my old friend. You're buried deep, but you're there."

She turned in silence to her still fuming son.

"We must start preparation for the rituals," she said. "This has to be done very carefully. No more mistakes from the three of you."

She glared at her son. The other two, standing at the entrance of the room tried desperately to look like shadows on the wall.

"Yes. Mother." Tenga said through gritted teeth.

Mr. Sunshine was not happy.

There were no sunny spots. No cushions to stretch out on. No food. He couldn't even get out of this small box.

That's not even counting the fact that there were all the strange creatures grabbing him and carrying him around in small boxes, and his creature was nowhere to be seen.

The box kept bouncing and getting jostled around, which made his mood even worse. His normal indifference to the world around him had faded into his other mood - dissatisfaction. He made the dissatisfaction growl.

At last the creature carrying his box put it down and soon another creature was peering in at him. He locked eyes with the creature and prepared one of his more emphatic dissatisfaction growls, but it never left his throat.

Those eyes.

Something familiar stirred within him. It wasn't a memory, or even a feeling. It was something deep, deep down inside. Something automatic, like hunting. Those eyes were... he wasn't sure. They were the opposite of his favorite patch of sunshine on the floor. They were the opposite of his favorite part of getting his chin scratched by his creature - the part where it feels so amazingly good he just has to bite the paw of the creature to show his appreciation. That never went well. The creature can't take a compliment.

Mr. Sunshine's hackles rose and the growl stifled earlier made its way out. This was all wrong. He didn't know what or why, but it was bad and he needed to be someplace that was better than this.

He needed a sunny spot in the worst possible way.

Jack was not happy.

But the misery brought on by the events of the last couple of hours was beginning to fade very reluctantly. Though his gloom did its best, it just couldn't compete with walking through the streets of the Scalayan city at sunset. Wonder and awe slowly took the place of the gloom, though nervousness and anxiety were still firmly in place. But even they took a second to enjoy the view. It was absolutely indescribable.

So here's a description:

As they walked along the streets, the branches of the buildings and/or trees (Jack still wasn't sure) arched overhead. In some places the limbs and leaves completely covered the path they took and in those places there was a faint glow emitting from within lighting their way.

The sky…

Where you could see the sky, as the last of the blue sun disappeared, the stars - thicker than Jack could have ever imagined - began to appear. You could still see the Scalayans as they flitted about in the skies above, their scales now glinting from the starlight above.

Jack wondered if there was a moon.

If there was a moon, and he had a girlfriend and brought her here - once she got over the shock of visiting another planet, dragon-looking aliens, sorcerers, etc., - he wouldn't need a cat. The view would be worth a thousand cats.

Jack smiled slightly, then felt a pang as he thought about Mr. Sunshine.

Suddenly, the spell of the view faded a bit. It was still amazing, but it was tempered by why he was really here. Just ahead of him Jal, Orlo and UFO Bob were busy chatting away. Bob was peppering them with questions and they were doing their best to keep up with the answers.

"...the cities were - grown, I guess you'd say - by the Scalayans to accommodate the Methens and others who were seeking refuge," Orlo was saying. "They've been amazingly hospitable in sharing their world. I think it comes from their history of not having a permanent home."

Jack realized he'd probably missed a wealth of information about this world, the people and the situation they were in. He also realized it would have made no difference. He was pretty much at saturation level with new experiences and information.

But there was one thing he wanted to know.

"Where exactly are we going?" He asked once UFO Bob stopped to take a breath and there was a break in the rapid-fire questions.

"Up there," Jal pointed to a spire they were walking toward. It seemed to be the highest one around. "That's where the ruling council meets. They're waiting for us."

Jack was a little apprehensive. The spire was very tall and, knowing the way everything else was going today, he was sure the meeting would be at the very top. He wasn't fond of heights. But he also thought about what the view would be like from so far up.

They continued to walk and Orlo and UFO Bob went back and forth with a furious pace which Jack decided to not even try and follow. As they walked, Jal lagged back a bit and ended up walking beside him. It was a moment before he noticed. He looked at her and the dim light from the tree/buildings shone off her dark hair and slightly illuminated her face.

43

He realized she was rather beautiful.

"Are you holding up okay?'" she asked, her voice about as soft and caring as it had ever sounded, which was just a peg or two down from drill sergeant.

"I know this is a lot for you to take in. We generally try to stay away from races that don't realize there are others out here. At least on a large scale. If we make contact, it's isolated. We find that if anyone we contact decides to tell, the other members of his species usually think it's some kind of mental disorder."

"Well that's... that's terrible. You know this and still contact these people? People like me and UFO Bob?"

Jal just shrugged.

"It's just part of it," she said. "At least on your planet they won't kill you for saying anything about it. At least as far as we've seen.

"Some aren't so lucky. So don't worry."

Jack suddenly realized Jal was trying to be reassuring but was doing it very badly. But he also felt as if she thought she were doing a good job. Maybe it was just a difference in Human and Methen cultures he decided.

"I feel better already," he said drily enough where he got it, but he was sure it would sail past her.

She smiled slightly, or maybe just scowled a little less, then pounded him on the back.

"Glad to hear it."

And they walked on in silence.

They finally reached the base of the spire and what he thought would be some sort of elevator to take them to the top. But it was not some sort of elevator. Not in the least. It was nothing. No cramped cubicle to all pile into. No buttons to indicate the different floors that the annoying person who used the elevator previously pushed all of before they got out. No close door button that didn't actually do anything. Nothing. At least as far as Jack could tell, though it looked very much as if there should be something there.

"How do we get up there?" he said, craning his neck to see up the sheer face of the structure.

Jal moved closer to him.

"It's probably best just to show you," she said. He felt her grab his hand and pull him forward. Out of the corner of his eye he saw Orlo take Bob's arm and move him in the same direction.

The sensation was sudden and unnerving. The four of them left the ground at an astounding speed heading up the side of the spire supported by nothing other than the fact that gravity apparently decided to look the other way for a moment.

For a split second Jack was too stunned to react. Then instinct took over. He realized the same was probably happening to UFO Bob, but the reactions were completely different.

Scalayans, in addition to having amazing vision, heightened sense of smell and a host of other senses (some of the 14 to 20 we discussed earlier) far better than anything humans have, also have very sharp hearing. (Editor's Note: The organs Scalayans have that humans, and some of the more pedestrian species of the galaxy, would refer to as 'ears' are really quite complicated since the species evolved in space, where, supposedly, no one can hear you scream. I won't bore you with the sciency stuff. Just know: Things happen and they work.)

As a result, at that particular moment, dozens of Scalayan heads turned toward the direction of Jack, Jal, Orlo and UFO Bob because they actually could hear a scream. They might have heard it even if they had been in space. It was an epic scream and one Jack would wish for the rest of his life he could either forget or take back. Or both.

But his scream wasn't the only sound. After the initial shock, there was a series of "Wheeeees," Woooooooos" and "Yaaaaaaaaahs!" coming from UFO Bob as he and the rest of the group shot up the side of the spire apparently on nothing but thin air.

The trip was only seconds, but to Jack seemed an eternity. Finally, he realized they were all standing on a large landing near the top of the spire. His throat hurt. His knees were wobbly. He really wanted to throw up, but the view was absolutely stunning and he realized Jal still had his hand and was speaking.

"That wasn't so bad was it?"

Once he was sure he wasn't going to vomit, Jack said without much oomph: "Maybe a little bit of a warning next time?"

"Wow!" UFO Bob said, gasping for air with a smile on his face. "That was fun. Can we do it again?"

Orlo simply turned away from the others and started walking into the opening in the face of the spire.

"The meeting room is back this way," he said. The other three started following.

Looking around, Jack couldn't tell whether the spire was a natural formation, artificial or something that had been grown. It looked like it could be all three. He thought about asking, but before he could, they arrived at a door.

A big door.

A dragon-sized alien door, Jack thought.

The door opened much more swiftly than Jack would have expected and beyond was a large chamber with a collection of different creatures inside, including two Scalayans. As the door opened heads turned. One of the creatures - which to Jack looked like something out of a nightmare with shiny black dermal plating, lots of different limbs, claws and teeth almost everywhere - started moving quickly across the room toward them.

Its maw opened, showing several rows of what appeared to be razor-like teeth.

Jack stood still, wanting to run in fear, but also knowing he probably wouldn't have a chance of getting away from this thing.

It came to the group and singled out UFO Bob. Several limbs snaked out and grabbed him.

"Bob!" the creature squeaked as it pulled the other human into what was now obviously a hug.

"It's so good to see you again! It's been too long!"

Sixth

Zola returned to her private chambers, the cage containing Mr. Sunshine floating in behind her and settling on a nearby table. There was still the occasional growl coming from the cage. Mr. Sunshine was still very unhappy, but was also getting bored. He let out the occasional growl or hiss to let anyone know about his ill temperament, just in case they forgot.

She touched a contact on the table where Mr. Sunshine settled, then looked back into the cage. The cat still glared at her in that angry-yet-bored manner only cats can manage. She probed his mind again and felt the familiar seed deep inside. Maybe it wasn't enough she thought. Almost five millennia had passed on Earth. Too many generations of Utu Lu's descendants had come and gone. The portion of the soul remaining may be too small.

She reached deeper. As she did Mr. Sunshine tried to move further back in his cage, but couldn't. Something was happening. He didn't know what, but he knew he didn't like it. It wasn't food. It wasn't a sunny spot and he definitely wasn't getting his way.

His growl grew more intense as Zola probed further. It was there. She felt she could almost reach out and grab it. If it hadn't been so diluted, reviving her old familiar's soul would be easy.

At that moment a door to the chamber opened and a young Methen woman entered carrying a tray. She said nothing but shuffled over and placed it on the table in such a way that showed she would have preferred to be anywhere else than where she was and with anyone else other than who she was with. It was a complicated method of shuffling developed through generations of slavery, well disguised to look just like ordinary shuffling.

She stood there, head bowed and eyes down, awaiting for Zola to speak. The sorceress looked at the girl. She'd grown to loathe the Methens. Before she'd taken their world, they were warriors. Defeated warriors brought to their knees by the Xanthians, but still possessing the hearts of warriors.

But time had passed and now, they were a race of slaves. Any shred of their valiant past was nothing more than a hazy racial memory. But as slaves, they were useful and would soon be more useful than even they could imagine.

It would take many Methen lives, thousands - maybe tens of thousands - to revive the soul of Utu Lu, but it didn't matter. She'd use them all if she had to. Her powers had reached their limit on their own. She needed her familiar to strengthen her bond with the magical beyond.

She waved the girl away and watched her retreat. That's the problem with Tenga, she thought. I left him to be raised by these mewling beings. Their submissive nature had rubbed off on him. She'd taken great care to make sure it was a trait she did not acquire from them as well.

Since there was no other choice over the millennia, from time to time she'd utilized various Methens to satiate any physical desires. But with very few exceptions, she'd found them all barely adequate.

When she'd been younger, she'd reveled in each new lover. But there had only been one who had - almost - been her equal. She'd even almost felt affection for him when they were still on Earth even though they were obviously forming up on opposite sides. He didn't have her raw power or her drive. Even then. But he had still been formidable.

A sly smile crossed her lips as her mind flashed back to those times.

Zola moved to the tray the servant had placed on the table and uncovered it revealing a plate of food. She paused for just a moment, then picked up the plate.

"I'd let you out to eat," she said to Mr. Sunshine, "but I don't think that would be a good idea right now."

She held one hand out toward the cage, palm forward. The door started to open and as it did, Mr. Sunshine saw his chance, but something was holding him back. Zola slid the plate of food in and the door closed. Mr. Sunshine felt the invisible hand release him.

Food!

Mr. Sunshine tore into the bowl of strange yet tasty food in front of him, giving it all his attention save the slight bit he needed to continue growling while he ate.

Meanwhile, about five thousand years ago - give or take a day or two - in ancient Sumer, during a convenient flashback, a young orphan was born in the city of Kish.

The infant, whose parents both died nearly a year before her birth - it's a long story involving magic, aliens and a mysterious crystal used to manipulate time, but it's rather dull - was placed in the care of the Goddess Kheba, who raised her as her own and taught her from an early age the art of saloon-keeping.

This became a prime education for the young girl. Lots of people all across the land of Sumer were more than a little interested in a tavern run by a goddess, even if the home brew was a bit watery and the appetizers somewhat overpriced.

Zola, as she eventually became known when Kheba decided she was worthy of a name, soaked in everything she heard from travelers who visited the tavern. She reveled in their tales of far off lands and became especially interested in the stories of magic. No wandering magician, no matter how skilled or unskilled, could leave without young Zola pumping them for information. She learned everything they would teach her and, once she'd mastered the fundamentals of mind control by the age of 10, she learned everything else they knew and began building her own little following over the next decade.

Eventually, Kheba grew worried over her adopted daughter's inclination to the darker side of magic. She contacted the High Council of Babylon who sent a young sorcerer named Barriantheluminous to Kish in order to bring Zola under control. After a battle of wills, magic and a drinking contest - all of which lasted for weeks - followed by an ill-advised fling which lasted days and ended badly, Barriantheluminous and Zola were left at an impasse.

It was at this point Kheba lost interest in human affairs after a dashing young sky god came to Kish. While the people of the region knew Teshub as a sky god - and he never exactly said he *wasn't* a sky god - he was actually an Octonian. After a whirlwind romance Kheba left Kish, Sumer and the Earth with Teshub and his traveling companion Illuyanka - who was a Scalayan working with Xanthol pirates looking to plunder the riches of some of the more uninteresting parts of the galaxy.

When Illuyanka became aware of the powers of both the young Zola and Barriantheluminous, she sent word back to her comrades that the two might become useful tools. Pirates can always use a good wizard or two.[1]

Several thousand Earth years later, which are also several thousand Scalayan years and Xanth years and Methes years as well, just not the same number, Jack knew none of this. Which

---

1 EDITOR'S NOTE: If this sounds nothing like actual history and more like I just went to Wikipedia and got a bunch of random names and facts gleaned from skimming an article on ancient Sumer then that's totally because over the course of many millennia the truth of what really happened becomes lost to the ages. Besides, you can't prove otherwise. I'm always very careful to wipe my browser history.

was fine. It has nothing to do with his part of the narrative and is simply there to add some color and background to the story.

He stood off to the side of a rather large chamber that held a dizzying array of different beings. Upon entering the room, Jal made for one of the larger Scalayans who Jack was later told was named Zev and who was one a leader of some importance.

The being who had greeted Bob was a Xanthian named Kkkkgh, a scientist who had done extensive examinations of Bob during his previous abductions. He and Orlo took the two Earthers around and introduced them to a number of different beings. Bob was enthusiastic but Jack was a little overwhelmed. He always had trouble remembering names. Now he had to remember species as well, not to mention greeting customs. Bob stopped him more than once from grasping something embarrassing while reaching out a hand to shake.

Eventually Jack was able to drift off to the side of the room and just watch. It was fascinating. He would have never in a million years dreamt these worlds and these beings could have existed. They were all the stuff of science fiction. This would make an interesting book, he thought, and possibly, in a more lucrative venture, a movie or series on a prominent Internet streaming platform - if the price was right (We can talk later...).

Eventually, the group settled down and turned from their individual conversations to more serious matters at hand. Everyone, save Jack, gathered around Zev, who was obviously leading the gathering.

"We all know why we're here," came the Scalayan's voice in a much more gentle sound than Jack had expected from such a fearsome looking creature. "Zola has made her move and now has what is a potentially powerful weapon at her side - the Earth cat known to our new friends Bob and Jack" - Zev nodded in Jack's direction. Several heads and other extensions turned his way then back - "as Mr. Sunshine, but is in fact a vessel for the spirit of Utu Lu, her former familiar.

"This will make it necessary to move our plans forward. It's time we go past trying to undermine Zola's power on Methes and engage in more direct action.

"It's time to go to war."

This sent chills down Jack's spine as he realized just what was going on around him. It was a war council. These people - Scalayans, Xanthians, Methens, humans and others he couldn't exactly remember - were getting ready to fight, to kill and to die.

And his cat was at the center of it all.

Jack was pretty sure he was going to throw up.

Which led to a new problem. Where was the nearest bathroom? In fact, was there a nearest bathroom? When you had the diversity of species he saw in the room, how did you even handle bodily functions?

Then he looked at the three Scalayans. How...? he started to think to himself and stopped.

He didn't want to know.

There was a rising sound of voices in the room as most of those in attendance began to comment on Zev's statement. The clamor was almost overwhelming. Jack could tell most supported Zev's call to war, but there were plenty who seemed more cautious. Jal was arguing with two... Jack couldn't remember what they were... but they were obviously not in favor of an all-out war. Jal's face was growing a deeper orange as she argued vehemently. Orlo and UFO Bob were talking to a couple of other more human-looking members of the delegation, though in a much calmer manner.

The thought of a war - being fought over his cat no less - was strange and abhorrent to him. War wasn't unfamiliar. There had been plenty of them on television in his lifetime, but fought

53

in far-away places he'd never go to and playing out more like a poorly-written primetime drama on the evening news than anything else.

Now, he was with the beings actually planning a war and it seemed increasingly likely he would be directly involved instead of ignoring it on a screen while he read a book. It was too much.

Jack turned to the still open door and quietly moved outside. The debate, if it could be called that, was reaching a fevered pitch. He needed some distance. If for nothing else than to just get a moment's solitude. Finding a bathroom would also be helpful.

He wandered the halls they'd come through moments earlier, looking down a side corridor or two, but deciding not to stray too far off the beaten path. As far as he could tell, there were no other rooms, at least that he could see. Just more tunnels running through the heart of the spire.

He eventually found himself standing near the spot where they entered, staring out the huge opening at the lights of the city/forrest below. It was still such a beautiful sight. He was so entranced he actually didn't hear the soft sound of a Scalayan landing beside him. He jumped slightly when he saw T'ki standing next to him.

"I didn't mean to startle you," the Scalayan said.

"It's okay. I wasn't paying attention. This view. It's just so…"

"It never fails to amaze me what a beautiful world we live on. Even after centuries, at times, it still takes my breath away."

"And now it's all in danger," Jack said, suddenly becoming very glum. "All because of Mr. Sunshine."

"No, Jack. You mustn't think that."

Jack felt a soft reassuring pat on his shoulder and realized it was T'ki's giant tail giving a friendly pat and rub of his shoulder.

"These events were put into motion a long time before you and Mr. Sunshine came into the picture. Thousands of years.

"If anything, it's our fault for not doing more sooner. When we rescued Barry and the first Methen refugees, there was a great deal of debate as to whether we should take a passive or more active role in dealing with Zola. There was no clear consensus so we never confronted her head-on.

"Now, we have no choice."

There was a long silence.

"I don't know what I'm doing here," Jack said. "I don't think I'll be very helpful in a war."

"Maybe not," T'ki said, "but for victory, you need more than warriors. They're in there making plans now. Zev and the others are sending out the information to all Scalayans. You'll have a part to play and it will be nothing more than what you're willing and able to do. We'll ask no more."

"But what can I do? I sell photocopier paper. I don't see how that will be much help."

"I don't know what that is, but you're more than your job. And you mean more to Mr. Sunshine than any of us. There may be a moment when you may have to help him decide if he wants to be Utu Lu - the former familiar of the sorceress Zola - or Mr. Sunshine - your faithful companion."

Jack took this in and thought about it. Maybe there was more to him than even he thought. He might not be the stuff of heroes, but he could definitely be the stuff of cat owners.

"I guess you're right," he said. "Though maybe 'faithful' isn't the best description for our relationship. 'Useful indifference' might be more appropriate."

T'ki gave Jack a puzzled look, but it was a Scalayan puzzled look and the expression was lost on Jack. Facial

55

expressions, if a being actually has something which could be described as a face, as well as body language don't often translate to different species. But scientists are working on that.

Jack and T'ki stood in silence and watched the lights dancing across the darkened landscape below them. Far below them. And now that Jack realized just how far, he became exceedingly uncomfortable.

"It occurs to me," Jack finally said nervously. "There are no rails to keep someone from falling off."

He stepped forward gingerly and peered over the edge.

"It doesn't seem very safe. It would be easy to fall off."

"It's not a problem," T'ki said.

Jack felt a pressure on his back and before he knew it he tumbled over the edge. But before he could even scream he noticed he was simply floating back to the ledge. After a second, he moved a foot forward onto the ledge and was standing on a solid surface again facing his Scalayan companion.

"See. Perfectly safe," T'ki said.

"You might have given me a little warning," Jack said, surprisingly calmly.

"Ah, but this gave you the opportunity to see just how you face the unexpected. And you did well."

Jack realized T'ki had a point. His heart was racing and he could feel the blood pumping in his ears. And even though there was an initial fright, he stayed relatively calm the entire time. He felt his confidence rise a bit. But he also went back to an earlier train of thought.

"Is there such a thing as a bathroom around?" He asked, realizing now that he was over the excitement of the moment, his musings were much more than academic.

Seventh

The war council went as such things go.

After some not insignificant time spent debating the merits of going to war, things began to calm down. A couple of members of the council left once it was clear there was no other path, but later returned once heads, or head-like appendages, had cooled down a bit.

Jack and T'ki wandered in, a short while after they left the landing, barely noticed. As it turned out, there were facilities humans would call bathrooms which are capable of adapting to any species' anatomical needs. The room was obviously roughly human-sized, so there was still the other obvious questions, but Jack, and his bladder, decided he didn't want to know the answer at this moment.

Editor's Note: While some may find it distasteful, the subject of handling the excretions of bodily waste amongst the vast number of species across the galaxy is a fascinating one, just from a technological standpoint. Not to mention the rituals and taboos different races and cultures may attach to the subject. One publication tried to tackle the subject but ended the effort after the twenty-fourth volume was published because almost no one actually wanted to read it. Maybe including full sensomatic Tri-D, video clips was a bad idea.

As a note of interest: Since Scalayans were and are a species that live in the vacuum and harsh conditions of space, they have a very effective anatomy. As a result, all their bodily waste is reused in one way or another. One use is the chemical plasma they produce.

You might not admit it, but you know you were wondering ever since Jack brought it up.

The beings gathered in the chamber looked at a number of charts and diagrams and other figures floating in the air. While Zev, the Scalayan leader Qol, and a third Scalayan Jack didn't know dominated the room physically, it was a human who had the attention of everyone.

Jack had never met this human leading the meeting, but he knew instantly it must be Barry, the wizard. He was not dressed in the same types of robes as his apprentice, Orlo, but in a dark formfitting suit. His head was completely shaved and his eyes seemed to gleam. The appearance was a little off-putting. Though he couldn't tell what, there was something strange about the man.

In time, the council ended and the plan for war was settled. Jack didn't follow much of what was discussed. The more he thought about what was to come, the worse he felt. As the crowd began to disperse, UFO Bob - who had taken an active role in the planning - made his way over toward Jack and T'ki. His excited grin was gone and, for the first time since Jack had known the man, he looked serious.

"I think we have as good a plan as we can possibly come up with," he said as he approached. "With any luck, Zola can be taken down with few casualties on both sides."

Jack didn't bother to ask what "the plan" was. He figured someone would tell him what to do when the time came. He tried to think of the right thing to say, but realized he didn't have any 'preparing for war small talk' in his repertoire. T'ki saved him from the awkward silence.

"Zev has been relaying the plans to us all so we'll each know our role. It is a good plan. He and Barry have done well.

"I see you're going in with the first attack wave, Bob. It's a very brave move."

Bob smiled in true modesty.

"Foolhardy maybe," he said. "But I hopefully won't actually be in battle. I'll be back with Orlo helping co-ordinate. I won't really be in the thick of it like you guys."

It took a second, but the 'you guys' part of UFO Bob's statement finally sank in. He looked back and forth between Bob and T'ki. Bob has a sheepish look on his face, as if he'd said something he wasn't supposed to. T'ki had apparently found something very interesting on the ceiling in the opposite direction of Jack that required her concentration.

"What do you mean 'you guys?'" Jack asked, a little concern growing in his voice. Suddenly, the confidence he'd felt earlier seemed to be slipping away.

"Um," Bob said. "Er," he added a second later. "Ahh...uh," he concluded.

He turned to T'ki who still seemed fixated on something that wasn't there.

"What do you mean 'you guys'?" Jack said, a bit of panic coming into his voice as he finally realized what 'you guys' meant and also suddenly realizing what T'ki's little shove from before was all about.

"Hey!" UFO Bob suddenly said a little too loud and nervously. "Here comes Barry! Let me introduce you."

Bob took Jack's arm and pulled him over toward the other human figure making its way towards them. As they drew closer Jack noticed Barry definitely looked odd. The back clothing didn't seem to actually be clothing and his skin looked oddly smooth. He was just about to ask Bob about it when they met.

"Hi Barry. This is Jack," Bob said quickly and nervously. "Jack, this is Barriantheluminous of Babylon, circa 3,000 B.C., lately of Scalaya by way of Methes."

"I…" Jack said.

"Um…" He continued.

"Wherewhenwhat?" He added.

"Just call me Barry," he said, extending a hand. Jack took it and as they shook, he came to the startling realization the hand wasn't real. Or, more precisely it was real in that it existed, it just wasn't the flesh and blood type of hand one would usually expect on a human.

Barry grinned as the realization came across Jack's face.

"Bob, I think someone forgot to mention to Jack exactly what I am."

UFO Bob let out an exasperated breath and slapped his forehead.

"Shit! I completely forgot. Sorry Barry. Sorry Jack. You see Barry was human, but thousands of years ago his body was injured beyond the Scalayan's ability to repair, so they placed his brain inside a simulated human form."

Of course they did, was what Jack thought.

"You're a robot?" was what Jack said.

Barry laughed a bit.

"No," he said. "Not as you know it. I'm organic, mostly. But my body isn't strictly human."

"Oh," Jack said. Why not, Jack thought.

Then, he thought again and turned to UFO Bob.

"What did you mean by 'you guys'?"

"Maybe we'd better go somewhere and talk," Barry said.

The altar had been built to the exact standards given to the Xanthian scientists and engineers by Zola. Thousands of Methen slaves had worked feverishly and quickly to build it in such a short period of time. It was a huge structure made in the same manner and from the same materials as its predecessor had been millennia ago on Earth. It was roughly pyramid shaped with terraces up the sides and a long, wide staircase going toward the top.

On Earth, the temple Zola had constructed existed on what she now knew was sort of a universal fault line. A spot where one could tap into the very surface of the background energy of the universe. Powerful stuff, but not as powerful as what she had modified her new temple to contain.

Power was what she both needed and desired. It would take one form of raw power to unlock the spirit of Utu Lu and restore her familiar, which would allow her to completely tap into and control the ultimate mystic power of the universe. She'd come close on Earth, but even with the universal background energy at her fingers, it wasn't enough. This time, she needed more.

This time she needed a black hole.

And nestled inside the temple was just that. A contained singularity which, at her command, would unleash its fury, consuming the temple, the ten thousand unsuspecting Methens and legions of her Zolanites - her faithful followers - who were willingly giving up their life forces for her.

Zola stood on a wide balcony overlooking the temple some distance away. The temple was massive, but it was dwarfed by the larger pyramid structure. One not built of stone, but of strong, exotic materials she would have never dreamed of so long ago in Kish. This was her fortress. It was where she would rule the stars. Possibly forever. How potent unlocking the mystical universal energy was, she didn't know. But once it was hers, she would see the stars burn out and be reborn over and over again in her lifetime.

Everything was almost ready. Things were going exactly as planned, she thought. Nothing could possible go...

Tenga stepped onto the balcony with a grim expression on his face. He hated his mother and hated being around her. He especially hated bringing bad news. And he hated that he wasn't able to talk anyone else into bringing her this news.

"What is it Tenga?" Zola said without turning to her son. Her voice was soft. Almost gentle.

"We have news from Scalaya. It seems a massive force is building there. We expect the first of them to emerge into our space in a day."

Tenga cringed inside expecting an explosion of anger from his mother. He'd borne her wrath many times for far less worse.

"Have you deployed our defenses?"

"Yes Mother," he said. "Strykers are deployed in standard defense formations. We have a fleet hidden with glamours behind the moon ready to close from behind. Ground troops are being deployed to protect the fortress and the temple.

"If our intelligence is correct, and I suspect it is, we'll outnumber them three to one in ships and ten to one in personnel.

"And, apparently Barriantheluminous along with Zev will be leading the forces into battle."

Zola turned. Her face was calm. Almost pleasant looking. Tenga had never seen this look before. Never.

"Thank you Tenga," she said gently. "You've done well."

He was at a loss. In his entire life, this was probably the kindest response he'd ever gotten from his mother.

She moved across the balcony toward him and he almost wondered if she was going to give him a hug. He shuddered slightly. But, she stepped over to the cage containing the cat and ran her fingers along its side.

He hated that cat too. It was almost comical, he thought, that she cared more for the damned creature - the cat he'd been tasked with retrieving - than her own son. Almost. Tenga knew good and well what that cat meant. He was fully aware the usefulness of just about every mortal in Zola's sphere was about to vanish. Simply being her son wouldn't make him any more or less valuable or disposable.

Tenga would have liked nothing more than to toss the cat off the balcony. He wondered if it would land on its feet.

"It will be good to see Barriantheluminous one last time," she said softly. Almost lovingly. "He was the one person who actually came close to challenging me in power. And he was the only man who was ever even a halfway decent lover."

Tenga cringed.

"Ugh! Mom!"

No matter how evil and powerful a sorceress your mother is and how much you loathe her, there are just some things a kid doesn't want to hear their parent say.

"I know I haven't been a real mother to you Tenga," she said. Mr. Sunshine stared out of the cage at her. His growling had pretty much stopped, but his eyes glistened with resentment. Even more now once he saw Tenga.

"And the simple fact is I had no desire to be a mother to you. I needed a child. I have trained you, to a point, in the ways of magic because I needed a tool. I needed a backup in case something were to go wrong before I reached the day when Utu Lu could be returned to me.

"You would have been a vessel for my spirit. Your own soul would have been obliterated and I would have occupied your body. Not my first choice, but it would serve."

Though he'd never been told exactly why he'd been brought into existence, he knew it was part of his mother's plans. But he'd never thought it was something like this.

"After today," she said, still gently, but with ice in her words, "I'll no longer need a back up plan."

There was silence for a moment. Tenga opened his mouth to speak, but she spoke first.

"Don't worry, my son. There's no need for you to fear. Though many will die today, you will not be one of them. I may no longer need you, but you are my flesh and my blood - even if you are tainted."

Tenga scowled. How many times had he heard those words come from her. Tainted. She'd always despised him for it and he knew good and well this might be his last day despite her reassurance. What better time to unload than when you're facing certain doom?

"Mother," he said barely hiding his rage, "I'm tired of the contempt you've show for me all my life. You are the one who decided to mate and produce a child with a Methen. I've known for a long time I meant little or nothing to you as a person. I just wish for once you'd tell me the truth!"

He expected fury when Zola turned suddenly and faced him. But instead of ire, he saw a softness he'd never seen. Not directed at him though.

"Very well," she said softly. "You'll have the truth.

"I have no plans to kill you. I do plan on giving you a world to rule once I come into my power. If you survive the battle. I plan on giving you my home world of Earth. It will be yours to do with as you please."

Tenga felt some relief, though it was tempered by his still strong hatred for his mother. But he was also curious.

"Earth? Why Earth?"

Zola smiled. It was a cold smile and one he knew well. Here it came. The real truth. And the pain that would come with it.

"Nostalgia," she said feigning lightness. "At least a bit. It's my home. I know you've never really been there - other than your trip to return my Utu Lu - but once this world and its people are used up, it will be the closest thing to a home you have."

Tenga let out a sarcastic laugh.

"Just because you came from there doesn't make it anything like my home."

64

A cold smile crossed her lips.

"Oh, not just me. You see there's another lie I've told you your entire life. A secret I've kept."

His mother didn't have to say another word. He knew. His own face became an icy mask of rage.

"Mother…" he said softly.

"Yes. Your father wasn't a Methen. It was bad enough using those vile beings for sex when needed. I'd never debase myself further by carrying one of their children."

Tenga turned away from her and closed his eyes.

"So you don't hate me for being part Methen," Tenga finally said. "You hate me because of him. My father."

"What is hate but a form of love," Zola said casually. "If I've ever loved, it was him."

He heard his mother walk across the chamber. The conversation was over. Her job was done. His psyche was devastated and she knew it. It was how she kept him in line. Much the same way she'd kept the Methens and her Zolanite followers in line.

But now things were different. Or maybe not different, but clear. Deep down inside, he'd never really felt the deferential nature of the Methens as part of his own. But he'd been lied to about his heritage his entire life, so he ignored that spark inside. Hidden it from a young age so his mother wouldn't see.

He wouldn't be able to hide it any longer, just like his mother wouldn't be able to hide the truth. He couldn't trust her word that she had no plans to kill him or that he would be set to rule Earth once she'd taken power. Tenga knew his best bet was to disappear. He had the plan. Now it was time to put it into action. His mother's new revelations made that crystal clear.

"Thank you Mother," he said after a long silence. "Thank you for finally telling me the truth. And, if I do survive the battle, it will be an honor to rule one of your worlds."

"Think nothing of it my son," she said. A thin smile crossed her lips. "Now, go and make sure our forces are up to their task. I'm counting on you to ensure the success of this ritual."

Tenga nodded and then turned and exited the balcony.

Once he was gone, she strode over to the cage containing Utu Lu and placed her hand on top of it. Even through the cage she could sense the power inside her former familiar. He'd had time to soak in the energy of this place and she could feel the spirit churning within him.

His emersion would be glorious.

She turned back to the door her son had exited through and a scowl crossed her face.

"Fool. As though I'd let you or anyone rule anything in my new domain. You'll be part of the fodder my empire will be built on, just like your father.

"But, you are competent when it comes to military affairs. You'll defend this world well and maybe you will be lucky enough to die in the battle, before your soul can be used to bring back my Utu Lu."

Well, Zola thought. A war complicates things, but death and destruction on the scale coming would do nothing but make her stronger during the ceremony. It really didn't matter whether Tenga and the troops were successful or not. Death was all that mattered. The Scalayans had inadvertently done her a tremendous favor.

It was perfect.

Now, nothing could possibly go…

Eighth

Wrong?"

Jack had asked that question at least a dozen times since he'd been told of his part in the plan. Zev, T'ki, Barry, UFO Bob and Jal had been very certain in their answers that, no, nothing could possibly go wrong. Probably.

Jal had been more forceful about it than the others. Jack's arm was still sore.

Some time had passed since the war council. Jack couldn't say exactly how much. A day or two at least. He saw little of UFO Bob. He spent most of his time with Jal and T'ki. Jal attempted to teach him some basics of fighting hand-to-hand, but pretty much decided it was useless so she spent the time teaching him how to use different weapons, environmental suits and shields.

They were all fairly easy to use and Jack had little problem learning, though he hoped he would be able to make it through the conflict without firing any weapons. It wasn't like some of the sci-fi shows he grew up watching. There was no 'stun' setting.

Though he saw little of Scalaya during this time, when he got the chance he would sneak out to the platform near the top of the spire where he'd been living and training to take in the sights. He wasn't really sure exactly how long it had been since he'd arrived because his internal clock had pretty much been pounded quiet, torn from the bedside table and thrown out the window. He finally decided to call any period of wakefulness between snatched sleeps a 'day.' If that was the case, starting from his arrival on Scalaya, which had definitely been night, it was now the third day.

In fact, it was dawn of the third day and Jack had been fortunate enough to wake up a little early and get to his favorite viewing spot. Up until then, the sunset when he'd first arrived had been the most spectacular thing he'd ever witnessed. Sunrise almost put it to shame.

Watching a blue giant star come up over the horizon is, in itself, pretty spectacular in most cases - actually all but three cases in the known universe - but watching it slowly illuminate the sheer beauty of the surface of Scalaya... well, it actually brought a little tear to Jack's eye. Not that he would have admitted it to anyone. Especially T'ki, who had silently settled beside him on the ledge.

"I'm beginning to think you're becoming somewhat enamored of our world," T'ki's voice popped into his head. Jack jumped slightly, then felt a slight pressure on his shoulder as the Scalayan laid its tail reassuringly on his shoulder. At least that was the intent. It's hard for a creature of that size and fearsome appearance to do anything reassuringly.

"I've noticed you sneaking out here to take in the view every time you get the chance."

"It's still hard to really comprehend," Jack said. "It's beautiful. And I'm still trying to wrap my head around being on a strange planet, meeting all the different types of beings I've met."

He paused for a second in awe as the light from the sun began striking some of the crystalline leaves below.

"Not to mention the whole magic and my cat being an evil sorceress's familiar or whatever."

"Yes. I can see where that might be a little hard to take in all at once," T'ki said reassuringly. "But you seem to be handling it well. At least Jal thinks so. Though I understand you've encountered a few awkward cultural differences."

Jack shook his head and put his hand to his forehead.

"She walked in on me in the shower," Jack grimaced in embarrassment. "And then asked which quarters UFO Bob and I would be sleeping in so she could join us."

Jack looked up at T'ki. He was becoming a little more used to their expressions and body language. He was pretty sure the Scalayan was amused with him.

"Lots of races co-sleep," T'ki said. "Methens and Scalayans both do. Xanthians don't. Though they do have five sexes, which makes their mating interesting."

"I'll bet," Jack muttered.

"You should see it some time," T'Ki said casually. "It's quite fascinating. Just ask any of the ones around. I'm sure they'd be glad to let you watch the next time they mate."

Jack felt his face grow flush and he cleared his throat nervously.

"I'll pass, thanks," he finally squeaked.

The tail patted him lightly on the shoulder.

"I'm sorry," T'ki said. "I didn't mean to embarrass you. Other than Barry, we haven't been around many humans. Bob fills us in on some things, but there's still a lot we don't know and aren't used to. I forgot your people are generally squeamish about mating."

Jack swallowed. This would have been an awkward conversation to have in just about any instance, but when it's with a huge, scaled, winged, fire-breathing alien, it tends to take awkward to an entirely new level.

"Not squeamish," Jack said. "It's just we generally practice a higher level of privacy than seems normal around here."

T'ki rocked him gently with its tail.

69

"I like you Jack," T'ki said. "You're kind of cute for a non-Scalayan. It's sad you can't be my mate, but you'd make a nice pet to keep around."

"Thanks?" Jack said uncertainly, slowly turning his head away from T'ki and back to the landscape below.

There was a punch on his shoulder from T'ki's tail and a growl that almost sounded like a chuckle.

"And I thought humans were supposed to have a sense of humor," T'ki said. Jack felt both relieved and even more embarrassed. He tried to say something, but nothing emerged when he opened his mouth, so he just stood there looking out at the increasingly day-lit landscape.

They both sat in silence for a few minutes, then T'ki began to move.

"Better go back inside," T'ki said. "It hasn't been announced yet, but today's the day. You'd better grab something to eat and then find Jal. It's going to be a long one."

Suddenly Jack felt the bottom of his stomach fall away. Up until now, the idea of going into war had just been theoretical. But that was about to end. He wasn't really sure how he felt about that.

But Jack was sure how he felt the first time he saw a proper spaceship.

The Scalayans needed no ships. The Methens had no ships, only the transport pods towed by the Scalayans. Most of those were small, but some could hold several dozen people. None were armed, though all had quite well-stocked bars.

When time came to leave Scalaya, Jack expected to be loaded into such a pod along with Jal and Orlo in order for T'ki to take them to their destination. But when the time actually came, Jack walked up on a group that included Jal, Barry, UFO Bob and T'ki on one of the landing pads. They were having a serious discussion that ended abruptly when Jack walked up.

It's always a bad sign when the giant monster, synthetic human wizard, alien warrior and multiple alien abductee quickly end a conversation when you approach.

"What's wrong?" Jack said, suddenly dismissing the previous reassurances he'd been given over the past three days.

"Nothing's wrong Jack," Bob said, placing a hand on Jack's shoulder in what was supposed to be a reassuring manner, but ended up being awkward because he was slightly too far away to do it comfortably. It's amazing just how often an appendage placed on a shoulder that's meant to be reassuring, for the races that do that sort of thing, has just the opposite effect.

"No, nothing except Barry is changing plans at the last minute and not telling anyone but us about it," Jal said not bothering to even try hiding the anger - which she was really bad at anyway.

"Changing plans? Which plans?" Jack felt a little panic. Improvisation was not his strong point. He always had to put a lot of planning into making things up on the spot.

"I'm coming with you instead of Orlo," Barry said. "And Bob has volunteered to take my place, going into battle with Zev."

"What!? You can't be serious?"

Jack looked at Bob.

"I mean the part with Bob, not the part about you going with us, Barry. I'm fine with having a very powerful wizard going with us - no offense Orlo. In fact, I'm ecstatic about it. But why are you taking his place Bob? You don't know how to lead troops into battle."

"Don't worry Jack," Bob said taking a step closer and making his arm which was still sitting on Jack's shoulder more comfortable, which made things even more uncomfortable because neither Jack nor Bob were really sure how long a duration a comforting hand on the shoulder should last, but both were now sure they were well past that time.

71

"I've played a lot of Halo and Call of Duty. I know about war. And I've led plenty of parties on quests in both D&D and Warcraft. I can lead.

"I'll be fine."

Jack was going to argue, but he stopped. For the first time he realized Bob was actually his friend. A real friend. And this was important not only to the war, but to Bob. He sighed.

"I'm going to hold you to that," Jack said. "That you'll be fine."

Bob smiled.

"I'd better be off and find Zev," he turned and started to leave. "I wish you could see the armor I'll be wearing," he said to Jack. "It looks almost like an actual suit of armor, and I'll be wearing it, riding on the back of a giant dragon - sorry T'ki, no offense - going into an epic space battle.

"It's like a dream come true."

And with that, Bob strode away from the group.

Jack wondered if he'd ever see his friend again…

And the answer is yes. On toward the end of the story. Bob lives. So do all the main characters. They need to be around in case of a sequel.

By the way, SPOILER ALERT for the preceding paragraph.

Once Bob left, Jack turned back to the group. They were all still looking at him, silent.

"So, I guess I'm ready to go. Ready as I'll ever be. Ready, somewhat willing and passably able. All that kind of stuff," Jack said, getting a little nervous as the others watched him.

Silence.

"By the way, where our pod?"

Jal looked at Barry. Barry looked at T'ki. T'ki looked at Jal. And so on.

No one looked at Jack.

72

"Um…" Jack said trying to gain some insight into the mutual staring contest which seemed to be going on.

"Our pod?" He asked weakly.

"About that," Jal finally said. "Remember when I taught you the ins and outs of using an environmental suit?"

In the comic books, whenever a character is faced with a situation which makes them visibly nervous, you often see a speech balloon with the word "Gulp!" in it. Had this been a comic book - or a graphic novelization as it would be known today - you would have seen such an expression coming from Jack.

At first it was scary, but then Jack realized he was in a spacesuit, strapped on the back of a 20-meter long winged reptile, tearing through the atmosphere headed into space where he, a warrior, a wizard and something amazingly like a dragon were heading to another planet to fight another more powerful wizard in order to save both his cat and his universe.

Upon that realization, his fear faded.

And was replaced by sheer terror.

But it was still pretty cool.

The terror wouldn't last, Jack told himself, but he was pretty sure he was lying.

As the air thinned out and the planet receded more rapidly behind them, the knot in his stomach grew tighter. He was holding on to the harness, which attached him to T'ki, for dear life.

"Don't worry Jack," T'ki's voice sounded in his brain. "You're perfectly safe. It's scary. Especially your first time. Don't tell them I told you, but even Jal and Barry and pretty nervous right now."

"Thanks T'Ki," Jack said, or maybe thought. He realized he wasn't sure which. "I'm trying to get a grip. It's just I have this thing about heights. Actually, more about falling. Or more precisely, hitting the ground at really fast speeds and really hard..."

While he was rambling, the vista around them began to change as they exited the last of the Scalayan atmosphere and moved into orbit. The blackness of space and the brilliance of the sun were stunning, but what was even more amazing was the sight they were moving toward.

Jack has seen plenty of science fiction movies and TV shows with giant fleets of spaceships zooming around the screen. They never looked anything like the real spaceships men used to go into orbit or, at one point, to actually go to the moon.

This scene looked like it was out of a movie. One with a budget that would have made George Lucas drool.

He saw ships, dozens and dozens, spread out across the horizon. Ships of all sizes and designs.

"We put out a call to some of our friends," T'ki said. "We've had a dozen worlds send forces."

"That's a lot of ships," was all Jack could say.

"Hopefully it will be enough," Jal said. He couldn't see her face, but he could hear the worry in her voice. Jack knew they would be outnumbered from the beginning. That's why it was so important their mission succeeded before the fleet reached Methes.

"Orlo informs me the ships will be ready to jump in approximately one hour," Barry said. "Hopefully, that will give us enough time to complete our task."

"All right, T'ki," Jal said. "Let's go."

For a moment, they continued to head toward the fleet in front of them, then a hole opened up in space and they disappeared.

Ninth

It was surprisingly easy to jump close to Methes and get in close to Zola's fortress, Jack thought. Almost too easy...

Okay, kind of cliche, and you're probably thinking this is setting up some kind of big ambush and a battle that puts our heroes in peril and almost gives away their plan, but nope. It all went smoothly thanks to precision flying from T'ki and a lot of fancy spell work from Barry to hide them.

It's not easy to disguise a 20-meter Scalayan and three humanoids but Barry did it and it worked. At least well enough to get them within sight of Zola's temple and the pyramid which dwarfed it. The sight would have been chilling at the best of times, but these weren't those times. Just the opposite. And the sight before them was absolutely horrifying.

The area around the temple was crowded with people. Jack could make out throngs of Methens, all being herded up into groups by legions of others in armor and with weapons. He knew these were the Zolanites. Even though he'd been told roughly what to expect, it was still a sight beyond terrible. He knew if they weren't successful, all of these people would die. And they would just be the first.

"I see Zola," Barry said softly. "She's headed for the temple and she has Mr. Sunshine with her. We don't have much time."

Jack didn't see at first, but then he saw an opening forming amongst the throngs, much like Charlton Heston parting the waters in that famous movie he was in - Planet of the Apes. Then he saw the tiny, lone figure walking through the human corridor ahead of something floating behind he knew contained his cat.

"Right," said Jal. "T'ki and I will go and try and draw their attention. We'll join you at the temple when we can."

"Good luck," Barry said, as Jal turned to leave.

In a fit of overwhelming emotion, Jack grabbed Jal by the arm before she could leave. He pulled her into his arms and kissed her, letting all of his emotions built up over the past several days surge through his lips. He felt a shudder as Jal surrendered, willingly, into his embrace…

Nah, Jack just reached out and touched her arm as she and T'ki were leaving.

"Be careful," he said. He was shocked at her response.

Jal smiled. Ever so slightly.

"Thanks," she said. "You too."

Jack and Barry moved swiftly toward the mob and quickly blended in with the Methens. They could be seen now, but Barry had put a glamour on them so they would not be recognized. Jack was nervous, excited, scared, and a host of other emotions all at once.

His role in all of this was very simple, and very dangerous. He actually came up with it, surprising the others during their planning of the mission. The others wanted him along because of his connection to Mr. Sunshine. Jack would stay behind while the others went and did their part. He would watch and relay information to the others and be there once Mr. Sunshine was saved.

But once he heard the plan, Jack decided he wanted more direct involvement. And that put him right in the middle of the throngs of Methens being herded to their doom on Zola's altar.

"Are you sure you want to do this?" Barry said. "It will be quite dangerous, especially if things don't go as planned."

"No," Jack said. "I'm absolutely sure I don't want to do this. But I have to. And not just for Mr. Sunshine."

Barry turned and smiled.

"T'ki was right," he said softly. "There is much more to you than meets the eye."

He clapped Jack on the shoulder and they moved on.

It took several minutes, but they finally reached the outer edge of the mass of Methens. They were almost to the foot of the temple and back several feet from a line of Zolanites keeping the crowds in line. There was a hum of nervous conversation around them as the Methens questioned what was going on. They knew the temple was built for some sort of ceremony, but had no clue as to their part in it.

Jack watched and waited. Zola moved closer, her eyes fixed on the temple and the cage with Mr. Sunshine floating by her side. He looked at Barry and saw the ancient sorcerer was staring intently at his old adversary. Everything was ready. All they had to do now was wait for…

The concussion from the explosion blasted across the crowd. Some fell, others covered their ears at the sound, but all eyes turned toward the fireball which had erupted from the top of Zola's pyramid fortress.

Jack froze. This was definitely an explosion and a distraction, but it wasn't the one they'd planned on. As the smoke cleared, he could make out the outline of several ships hovering just above what used to be the top of the structure.

It took just a second for him to finally react, but Jack looked at Barry who then shouted "Now!" It was almost as if Barry's shout put everyone in motion. The crowd around them erupted into screams and shouts. Methens began to flee. Some decided it was time to actually try and turn the tables and they went after the Zolanites, who were just as startled to see a group of their own ships apparently attacking the fortress.

Just before Jack sprang into action, he saw Barry begin to glow. The wizard was chanting something and he could feel the power flowing.

Leaving his companion, Jack made his way as quickly as possible through the chaos as he could toward Zola. He never took his eyes off her or the cage. She was obviously stunned just like the rest of them, but it took her only a second to recover. Facing the ships above the fortress, she raised her arms and a beam of energy shot forward toward the lead craft. At the same time, another beam of energy shot forward from the lead craft and the two intersected.

As this happened, the other craft streaked away and headed straight toward Zola, firing similar beams of energy. More beams flew away from Zola, one striking a craft which burst into a large fireball. Jack knew this couldn't be Jal and T'ki. The other craft were firing indiscriminately. He saw Methens and Zolanites alike falling under their attack. Something else was up, but he was't sure what it was.

He pushed the thought out of his mind for now. He was closing in on Zola and her cargo. He knew Barry would strike soon and that would be his cue.

And strike Barry did.

Another blast of energy struck Zola from behind, knocking her quite a distance forward. From the corner of his eye, he saw Barry rise from the crowd into the air and swoop quickly toward the fallen sorceress. Jack ran as hard as he could to where Zola had been standing, grabbed the cage containing Mr. Sunshine and ran into the crowd.

The cage was much lighter than he thought it would be, which was great because it enabled him to move quickly through the crowd. Once he was a short distance away, he glanced down at the cage to reassure his friend, but his smile quickly faded.

The cage was empty.

Tenga was furious.

The idiot Sala had jumped the gun and fired on the fortress, thus giving them away before they could catch his mother unaware. He saw Sala pay the price as his ship erupted into a fireball, but he could do little more than try and make the best of the mess his former friend had made. He poured everything he had into the battle with her, but he feared now with the advantage of surprise gone, it was hopeless.

Except...

He saw a second blast of energy from the crowd hit Zola and her beam broke free from his. He quickly turned his craft and gave the command to the others to refocus their fire on Zola. He saw the other sorcerer, Barry, - his father - floating above the crowd, also closing in on her.

He had hated Barry and the Scalayans just as much as his mother for so long. But now...

Tenga shook the thought off. It didn't matter now. It might not ever matter. The man fighting his mother below obviously didn't know her secret. But he was a distraction and the enemy of your enemy...

Speaking of which, he also spotted a large Scalayan with a lone rider on its back streaking toward the chaos.

Ah, reinforcements, he thought. He hit a switch on his com.

"Scalayan, and who ever else is listening. This is Tenga, son of Zola. I'd really like to kill my mother, and since I want her dead far more than any of you ever could, maybe we can come to some sort of arrangement."

"Maybe you should talk to him," came T'ki's voice in Jal's mind. "This seems more up your alley."

Jal nodded, both mentally and physically and opened her com.

"Tenga. This is Jal with the Scalayan resistance," she made that up. They never thought about coming up with some cool-sounding code name for what they were doing, but it sounded good in a pinch. "We do seem to have the same goal in mind. Since you have busted up our plan, I assume you have one of your own?"

"We did," Tenga's voice came back. "But one of my lieutenants screwed it up pretty royally. We're improvising right now."

"Well the first thing you need to do is tell your men to quit firing on the crowd. We're trying to save the Methens, not blast them. Plus our people are down there as well."

"Yes. I've seen your wizard. He's not quite up to Mother's level, but maybe together..."

"Yes. Together," Jal said. "And don't decided to change your mind in the middle of all this. If you do, I'll hunt you down myself."

"I'm sure you would," Tenga said as condescendingly as possibly, but deep down inside, he could tell she could and would.

"Shall we start shooting Mother now?"

The battle raged on.

When Jack saw the cage was empty, he ran back to the spot he'd first grabbed it, thinking maybe Mr. Sunshine had gotten loose in the confusion. He knew it would be hopeless if he had. There was so much confusion his cat would surely be lost or...

He couldn't even think about it.

The ships above had changed position, as had Barry and they were all concentrating on Zola. The air sizzled with energy and was heavy with explosions, screaming, yelling and other weapons fire as the battles between the Zolanites and the Methens continued.

Jack stopped at about the spot where he'd grabbed the cage. Nothing.

He couldn't stay there long. There was fighting all around him. He heard an ear-piercing shriek and looked to the sky. He saw T'ki and Jal streak toward the battle with Zola. A blast of plasma spewed forth from the Scalayan and Jal unleashed the fire and fury of her own weapons.

Jack wasn't sure what he should do next. His part of the plan seemed to no longer matter. He felt sure with all the firepower concentrated on Zola, it would only be a matter of time. He knew he wouldn't be any help fighting the Zolanites, but maybe he could help the Methens.

He looked around. Bodies littered the grounds between the fortress and the temple. Fighting was everywhere as were people running away. He wasn't sure exactly where a safe place from the fray would be. He looked up at the temple and saw an opening near the top on a long flight of stairs on its side.

Maybe that would be a good safe place for people, he thought. Inside the giant, scary-looking temple the evil sorceress was heading to in order to perform some kind of ritual.

On second thought…

But before he actually made it to that second thought - and really, before he'd even completely finished the first - he felt something in his mind. A tingle that was both unfamiliar and familiar.

The thought suddenly came to him: Mr. Sunshine is already in the temple.

At that moment he heard a hum, rising in pitch. There was a flash followed by explosions of the ships above. Bodies flew through the air. He saw Barry go flying and T'ki plummet towards the ground. Then he saw Zola rise into the air.

Tenth

The first thing that went through Jack's mind was to grab a weapon. He'd had one when this all started, but in the mad press of people once the panic started, he guessed he'd lost it somewhere. He found one of the discarded Zolanite rifles and scooped it up as he ran toward the temple stairs.

As he mounted the stairs two thoughts came to him: First, he would be a very open target on the stairs if someone should take notice and care to start shooting at him. He hoped everyone else was too preoccupied in shooting each other to notice.

The second thought was the realization upon looking at the Zolanite rifle in his hands more closely, that he had almost no idea how to use it. There were a number of things which could have been triggers or settings. He knew which end to point away from him, but that was about it.

He tossed it aside.

Jack moved up the stairs as fast as he could, but it didn't take long for him to realize just how out of shape he was. He moved slower and slower and thought more and more about what an easy target he was.

A time or two he chanced a glance behind him. There was still fighting going on, but the tide had definitely turned against the Zolanites, which led some of the Zolanites to turn with the tide and join the Methens.

There was a glowing ball of smoke and flames in the spot where Barry and Zola were trading magical blows. He saw a figure running toward the conflagration and realized it was Jal. T'ki swooped down, unleashing a stream of plasma into the cloud.

Jack was getting closer to the top, which was good. He was short of breath. His legs and his lungs were burning, and he was getting a little light-headed. When he finally reached the opening into the temple, he stopped to catch his breath. He was higher than he thought. The fighting was still raging. He could only imagine what was going on inside the cloud surrounding Barry and Zola. Even from this distance he could tell it must be epic.

He also wondered about what was going on above the skies, in orbit of the planet where Zev and UFO Bob were leading the charge against a fleet of Zolanite ships. He hoped Bob was okay. He hoped they would all end up okay.

Jack turned toward the entrance. It was inky black just beyond. He still felt… something… pulling at him from deep inside. The sensation told him that Mr. Sunshine was somewhere down that corridor. The sensation also told him he was an idiot for going after the cat because it was most probably too late and, as a parting shot before Jack pushed the feeling away, it told him he dressed funny as well.

Jack took one last long breath and stepped into the darkness of the temple entrance.

The corridor was long and dim and descended at an angle which told him if he got momentum going forward, it would be hard to stop. Jack moved cautiously, but quickly. The entrance shrank behind him and after some time seemed to disappear. It was puzzling, but even though the temple was large, he judged the distance he'd travelled should have put him well beyond the far wall.

Jack wasn't sure how long he followed the corridor. Maybe ten minutes. Maybe an hour. He began to feel a little heavy, but brushed it off as fatigue. Adrenaline was keeping him going now. He really wished he could have a jolt from a candy bar and a highly caffeinated beverage right about now. He wondered if the Scalayans or Methens had anything like coffee. He'd been so busy the last few days, he'd barely paid any attention to the things he'd been eating.

Tea would also be good. Everyone had tea of some kind. Herbal would be fine, but something good and caffeinated would also be welcome. And a doughnut. He wondered if they had doughnuts. They probably wouldn't be called doughnuts, but he was sure if he described doughnuts to them, they would have something.

It was odd to think about the fact that even though Barry was human (sort of) he'd never had doughnuts or coffee. Or watched television, which probably wasn't a bad thing...

Jack realized his mind was wandering and had been for some time. What made him realize this was the corridor began to level out and there was a light up ahead. He paused for a second and then crept toward the light.

The corridor opened up into a large chamber. So large he could barely see the other side. So large it couldn't possibly be inside the temple. But it was. He suddenly realized the temple must be larger on the inside than the outside.

Where had he heard that before?

He shrugged the thought off.

In the center of the giant chamber was a blindingly bright sphere. He couldn't tell how far because at times it looked like it was actually beyond the far wall and in the center of the room at the same time.

As he stepped into the room his feet felt unusually heavy. It was more than fatigue, he realized. His body actually felt heavier than normal. By more than a little bit and in a way diet and exercise wouldn't fix.

As he puzzled over the new sensation, he noticed some movement ahead. Farther into the chamber he saw a dais slightly off to the side. Something was moving on top of it.

Jack staggered a bit under the new heavy sensation as he moved toward the dais. He couldn't yet make out what it was on top, but he knew. Somehow he knew.

You're just in time, human, came a voice out of the ether all around him. *You'll bear witness to the resurrection of Utu Lu and the birth of my reign over the cosmos.*

This must be Zola, Jack thought. But how?

Silly human, the voice cackled. *Even as I battle outside these walls, I'm also in here, moving toward my destiny. Every life that is extinguished outside these walls feeds the soul of my old familiar. Soon, he will emerge and allow me to capture the mystical power of the entire universe.*

Jack felt he should shout some defiant taunt toward the disembodied voice. Some boast of the victory his side was sure to achieve. Some bon mot which would have sounded good coming from the lips of John McClain to Hans Gruber.

He opened his mouth, but he had nothing.

There weren't more than a few yards between him and the dais now. He saw Mr. Sunshine sitting in the center, staring at the ball of light in the middle of the chamber. He was glowing and it looked almost as if his body was beginning to morph, just slightly.

"Mr Sunshine?" He said, timidly.

The cat turned his head. The eyes were glowing and suddenly Jack felt a spasm of pain shoot through his body. He convulsed and collapsed.

The cat you knew as Mr. Sunshine - which is really a stupid name for a cat by the way - no longer exists. The soul of my Utu Lu is rising. Consuming. And once he's done with your cat, he'll feast on you!

"No..." was all Jack could manage.

When the waves of pain stopped, he struggled back to his feet. He made a few steps toward the dais. He wasn't sure exactly what he was going to do, but he knew he had to do something.

"I won't let you destroy Mr. Sunshine," he gasped. "And it's not a dumb name. Maya named him that when he was a kitten. She thought he was a cute little puff of sunshine."

Ugh, came Zola's voice. *Your girlfriend sounds as stupid as that name.*

"She's not stupid!" Jack spat back, moving closer to the dais. "Plus, she's not my girlfriend any more. We broke up."

She dumped you, huh. Not surprised. You seem pretty pathetic.

"No, it was mutual."

Yeah, that's what people always say when they're the ones who get dumped. She left your loser ass. And she left you with the cat with a stupid name.

"And exactly what kind of name is 'Utu Lu?'" Jack shot back. He'd reached the edge of the dais. Mr. Sunshine seemed unaware of his presence or unconcerned. His fur crackled with energy. Jack could feel it tingling on his skin.

It is a name of power! The voice boomed. *It is a name which makes the entire world tremble. Which will make the entire universe bow down before it.*

"Yeah, got it," Jack said, sliding onto the dais, "but what does it actually mean? It's ancient Sumerian I take it?"

It is the language of High Sumer. The language the Gods spoke down to us when they gave us their power!

Jack reached out a hand toward Mr. Sunshine. The energy flowing off his cat was intense. The nerves in his hand and along his arm screamed. His muscles tensed from the pain. But he felt he needed to keep up the struggle. Keep Zola talking, maybe distract her just enough…

They mean... Zola's voice boomed, then went silent. Jack's hand was so close to his cat now.

They mean... Never mind! It doesn't matter. All you need to know is now you DIE!

Jack's hand touched the fur on Mr. Sunshine's head. His fingers were like burning lead, but he managed to get them to move.

And started scratching behind Mr. Sunshine's left ear. His favorite spot.

"Such... a... good... kitty..." Jack groaned through the pain.

There was a deafening boom. The room suddenly went dark and Jack felt the pain fall away instantly. He collapsed on the dais.

The next thing Jack knew he felt Mr. Sunshine bump his head against his forehead and the purring cat rubbed across his face, covering his nose and lips in fur. He managed to reach a hand up and rub the cat's head.

"That's a good kitty."

Then, there was total darkness.

It is interesting how history can sometimes echo. Certain themes seem to repeat over and over. Certain types of people come and go repeatedly throughout the ages. And certain attributes and descriptors seem almost embedded in the walls of the time/space continuum.

For example, if Jack had bothered to travel back in time to ancient Sumer, to the city of Kish and happened upon a tavern run by a goddess and a young girl, he might have noticed a fluffy, yellow cat. If he'd questioned the little girl about the cat, he would have discovered that cat's name was Utu Lu: Lu because the cat was male, and Utu because he looked like "a little ray of sunshine."

Eleventh

So this is my chapter!
It's me, Bob. Though some people call me UFO Bob.
I get it. I guess sometimes I can get a little obsessed. But I was right! It'd be nice to actually let people know I was right, but it's probably for the best they don't. Not sure most people could really handle knowing about what all's really out here.

Jack did okay, but it took him a while to get used to it all and he was thrown right into the deep end. In the really deep end.

But anyway, This chapter is about me! Back to the narrative.

The ride atop Zev from the surface of Scalaya had been awe-inspiring, though Bob barely had time to notice. From the time he donned Barry's armor, he was put in touch with every ship and every Scalayan gathered around the world. It was almost overwhelming, but he'd been learning the system for a while with the help of Zev and Barry.

He watched on his scope as T'ki and their passengers rose from the planet and then disappeared. That triggered the countdown for his fleet to ready their own jumps.

One of the logistical problems in having so many ships from so many different races and worlds is they all worked a little differently from one another. They all accomplished the same thing - getting somewhere very fast - but they did it in different ways. The Scalayans opened portals into null space, others used warp drives, hyper drives, slipstream drives, infinite improbability drives - you name it, someone uses it.

Timing was the key. Some moved a little faster than others. Some took great distances to get going and to slow down. Some just popped from one place to another in an instance.

It was up to Bob to make sure everyone left when they were supposed to and arrived when and where they were supposed to. It wouldn't do much good to have ships popping back into normal space inside one another.

Moments after the departure of T'ki, he gave the orders for the first ships to start moving to jump speed. He fed revised co-ordinates to other ships to give them plenty of room to re-emerge into the real world.

It was all very exciting, and very distracting. He barely had time to think about the fact that he was about to go into a space battle that was bigger than anything he'd ever seen in the movies. And more real.

Time went by quickly. He received a brief signal that told him T'ki and his team had emerged at Methes. More than half of the fleet was already on its way and it was time for the rest of them to leave. Hundreds of portals opened up as Scalayans and other ships began to depart. Bob took a glance back at the world behind him. It was beautiful.

He wondered how many of them would be returning.

There wasn't much to do in null space. Communications are limited, so he took the time to relax and to get ready for what was ahead. No one was sure exactly what kind of fleet they would be facing, but they all knew it was big. Much larger than the fleet flying in to oppose it.

His stomach tightened a notch.

"How's everything going?" A voice sounded in his ear.

It was Orlo.

He was riding Qol, the leader of the Scalayans. They would stay out of the fighting as much as possible and co-ordinate from behind the lines. Zev and Bob would be at the front.

"Fine as it can be," Bob said. "I'm getting a bit nervous."

"Me too," Orlo said. "I guess it would be bad if we weren't."

"I suppose."

Silence.

"You know," Orlo finally spoke. "When this is all over. I'd like to visit Earth someday. I've heard Barry talk about it quite a bit. It sounds like a nice place."

"Yes, definitely," Bob perked up. "I'd be glad to take you and show you around. Though I haven't been to most places there."

"Why?"

"Well, it takes more to get around there. No teleporting or spaceships or magic. It takes days to get from one side of the world to the other. And money.

"I've had the time, but never the money."

"That's a shame," Orlo said. "When I come, I can just take us where ever we want to go. No need for money. We can't teleport, but I can get us anywhere faster than days."

Bob was excited about the possibility. He'd always wanted to travel. He'd never been more than a couple of hours from home - except for space and other planets and such.

"That sounds good."

"Maybe Barry can go with us and we can go visit where he grew up."

"I'm not sure there'll be anywhere to visit," Bob said. "It's been gone for thousands of years."

"Shouldn't be a problem," Orlo said nonchalantly.

Before Bob could express his surprise at such an idea, the suit's systems came to life and he was starting to get data.

"We're just about to jump back into real space," Zev said. "We should come out well away from the Zolanite fleet, but be prepared for anything.

Bob wasn't sure he was prepared for anything, but he was prepared as he could be.

"Good luck Orlo."

"You too, Bob."

Real space came into bloom all around them.

Everyone was where they were supposed to be. Some were still at pretty sizable distances, but they would close ranks as they approached Methes.

As soon as they emerged, Bob got a ping from the enemy fleet. They were in close around Methes, but it was puzzling. It was only about half as large as they'd expected. Definitely much larger than the approaching fleet, but it still wasn't right.

"All units," his voice sounded in every ear in every ship and in every mind of every Scalayan. "Something's not right. There aren't enough ships around Methes. There has to be more somewhere. Maybe they've set a trap for us. It would be nice to know where they are going to try to spring it and what they're going to spring it with."

There was a great deal of chatter for a moment, then reports started coming in. Nothing. Nothing. Nothing. And even more nothing.

"They're somewhere I'm sure," Orlo said. "But if they're cloaked, it's a strong one. We've cast detection spells as widely as possible, but nothing."

"We'll have to go in blind then," Zev said. "But we know it's a trap. We'll keep all eyes open. Let's spread our formation so whenever they come, they won't find us bunched up."

Ships and Scalayans moved into new positions. Bob became very busy sending information about positions of both the attacking and defending fleets.

"Nothing from T'ki. Strange," Zev said to Orlo. "I can't get any sense of him or the others from Methes or anywhere around."

Bob swallowed hard.

"Could... Could they have been destroyed?"

"I don't think so," Zev said. "We would know T'ki's passing."

Bob felt a little relief.

"It's the planet," Orlo said. "We can't detect anything because there's a powerful force coming from the surface. Centered at Zola's fortress."

"Hopefully that's where they are and they're close to completing their mission," Bob said.

"We can only hope," Zev agreed.

Though the fleet moved into the Methen system well away from the planet and the other fleet, it didn't take very long for the two to get into range. The two mighty fleets moved closer and closer, neither making an overtly aggressive move toward the others.

"Zev! Bob!" Orlo's voice came through excited. "Something's happened. The force blocking everything is clearing.

"And there's a large fleet coming into focus behind us..."

The information popped up on Orlo's displays.

"Oh shit."

There was a slight pause. Then came Zev's voice.

"Oh shit, indeed."

While the Zolanite fleet ahead of them was much larger than theirs, the enemy ships now behind them numbered more than both fleets put together. As the news of this spread through the fleet, Bob was assaulted with a cacophony of excited voices.

It took a lot of calls to calm down, but the crews of the ships began to come to grips with the situation.

Zev gave orders to move the fleet into a defensive sphere. One that could spread out to attack, but still move in toward the planet. The Zolanite fleets moved to counter, both sides still seeming to wait for the other side to fire the first shot.

"Why haven't they attacked yet?" Bob pondered.

"I don't know," Orlo said. "And that worries me even more than if they had."

Ships moved on both sides, preparing to unleash a myriad array of deadly weapons upon each other. Tensions rose. Then something happened.

Bob wasn't sure what happened, but he felt it.

Everyone felt it.

It wasn't a physical force, it just felt like *something* happened.

Everyone was stunned. For a second.

Then something even stranger happened.

Bob received a signal from a Zolanite ship.

"Um, excuse me," the voice said. "Sorry to bother you, but we've all been talking it over and we've decided we'd rather not fight."

"What?" Bob was thrown rather off balance. Of all the things he'd tried to prepare himself for going into battle, not actually having to battle wasn't one of them.

"Why?" Was all he could think to say.

"Well" came the voice, somewhat unsure of itself, "we're really not sure. It's just all of a sudden, we feel like we really don't want to do this. Fight, I mean. We just want to go off and do something else.

"Myself, I'd like to start gardening."

"Well..." Bob was still somewhat at sea, "Are you sure?"

"About gardening," came the voice. "Oh yes. I've always been fond of it. I used to raise pomesas in a small garden at my parent's house. Not everyone likes them, but I think they're delicious. Lightly fried with some dunnum spice..."

"No," Bob said. "About the fighting."

"Oh yes," came the voice. "Yes. We've all talked it over and agreed. We don't all want to garden, but we're all sure about the fighting."

"Well..." Bob said.

"I mean, unless you really want to I suppose. Though I'm not really sure what we'd get out of it. Our hearts just aren't that into it any more. Not sure why."

"Well... okay then." Bob couldn't tell if what was going on was real. It wasn't until the Zolanite ships began to break formation, heading off in multiple directions, that it hit him.

"What's happening?" came Orlo's excited voice.

"I'm not sure," Bob said. "But I think the war's over."

There was a very long pause.

"Why?" Orlo finally said.

"I'm not sure.

"By the way. What are pomesas?"

Twelfth

The first thing Jack was aware of as he awoke from a long and dreamless state of unconsciousness was difficulty breathing. Something was partially blocking his nose and mouth. He wasn't completely aware yet. Still groggy. Whatever it was, it was warm. He raised his hand to his head. It was soft. It was… purring.

He opened his eyes to see the rear end of Mr. Sunshine covering the lower half of his face. He could feel the rest of the cat stretched out along his neck and upper chest. Jack's arms still felt like lead, but he managed to shift the cat off his face, then spent the next several minutes trying to get fur out of his mouth and nostrils.

Jack was beginning to regain his senses a bit. He sat up groggily and looked around. The chamber was dimly lit from somewhere he couldn't see. The light in the center of the chamber was gone but there was still something there, dark and formless. He didn't know what it was, but knew he needed to be as far away from it as possible.

He looked down at Mr. Sunshine, who had curled up next to him on the dais. He looked much more normal than before. Almost like his old self, just a bit more haggard. Jack still felt heavy and just a little dizzy. He realized he must have been unconscious for quite some time, but wasn't sure how long. He wondered what had happened to Zola. Was the battle still going on? Had they won?

It took some moments before he felt certain enough of his strength to move. Jack slid slowly, achingly over to the side of the dais and got to his feet. Mr. Sunshine looked up at him. He made a single "meow" and stood shakily. This had been an ordeal for him as well.

Jack scooped his cat up in his arms and headed back to the entrance to the chamber. Once there, he turned back and looked around again. It was quiet. His heavy breathing seemed to echo off the walls. It was time to leave. His part was done. He was sure of it. He turned and started back up the corridor.

It was a long walk. He had to pause several times to rest and he and Mr. Sunshine would just sit on the floor of the corridor until they could move on a bit further. After some time, Jack noticed he was beginning to feel better. His limbs weren't so heavy and his breath wasn't so labored. Even Mr. Sunshine seemed to perk up.

Eventually, the cat became a little restless in Jack's arms so he put him down and Mr. Sunshine walked at his own pace, never straying too far ahead or behind.

"Well buddy," Jack finally broke the silence, looking down at his orange-furred friend. "I guess we did it. Not sure what we did. Not sure how this is going to turn out, but we apparently did it.

"Now I wonder how we'll get back to Earth? I hope there's someone left to take us back..."

He suddenly realized even if they'd won, the cost might have been a great one. How many of his friends were dead? What price had the Methens, the Scalayans, everyone, paid? He felt a pang in his stomach. It was worry. It was also hunger. He realized he was starving. And thirsty. A cat bowl full of water was actually sounding pretty good right now.

He had been out a long time.

It must be just as bad for Mr. Sunshine, Jack thought. How long has it been since he's had food or water. But the cat seemed to be taking all of it much better than he was. And in fact, seemed to be getting just a little impatient as they sat on the cold, hard floor without a single patch of sunlight to be found.

Or was there?

Jack looked down the long corridor ahead noticed a pinpoint of light far in the gloomy distance ahead. They must be getting near the end. This perked him up and he started moving faster. After a while, when Mr. Sunshine didn't seem happy with the new non-leisurely pace, Jack scooped him up again and moved even faster.

The light grew slowly, but it was definitely the entrance. He could begin to see the sky outside. It looked as if it were daytime again. But how many days? Jack wondered if anyone had noticed him go into the temple. If the fighting was over, why hadn't anyone at least come in to check and see what Zola had been up to?

Jack broke into a trot and the entrance got closer. He finally got to the opening and stepped out onto the landing at the top of the stairs. Below him, he was surprised to see fighting still going on. Not like before. Mostly small pockets and even those were dying down as he watched. There were still thousands upon thousands of people on the grounds below. Some were lying injured or dead. Others were walking around in confusion. Further back toward the Pyramid fortress, now missing its top, he saw some familiar figures.

They were quite a distance, but he could make out Barry, Jal and T'ki standing around an inert figure, very nearly in the same spot he'd seen them when he entered the temple what he now figured to be days ago.

Confused and curious, he started to slowly make his way down the stairs. About halfway down, some of the Methens noticed him and started approaching the bottom of the stairs. When this started, apparently one of his friends saw as well. He saw Jal point and start running toward the temple. T'ki and

Barry stayed by the other figure he now assumed must be the body of Zola.

Obviously they had won. But how? And what had happened to him and Mr. Sunshine?

Though the heaviness he'd felt in the temple was gone, the steps were still a great deal of effort and all the time he'd spent without food and water had weakened him more than he realized. He was running on adrenaline but that was getting in short supply as he reached the bottom of the temple.

"Jack!" Jal shouted as she approached. She was actually smiling, sort of. "You're okay! And you have your cat. I don't know what you did, but it saved us all!"

She came up to Jack and embraced him awkwardly, which didn't make Mr. Sunshine very happy because he was caught in between. When she let go, Jack staggered a bit, almost dropping the cat. Hands reached out and steadied him.

"Are you okay?"

"Water," he croaked. He then sat down on the bottom step of the temple.

Some of the Methens broke away and returned a few minutes later with some water and food for both Jack and Mr. Sunshine. He drank deep and stuffed something into his mouth, he didn't know what it was, but he chewed it hungrily and swallowed before he spoke again. Mr. Sunshine sniffed the water and drank but before he ate the food he gave the distinct impression to all those around it was acceptable, barely, but he expected better.

Jal let him drink and eat for a moment before she spoke again. She'd been looking back to the others. Jack couldn't see too well, but what he thought was Zola seemed to be standing statue still. Methens had begun to crowd around both places, but others held the curious back.

"So what did you do?" Jal finally asked. "I saw you step into the temple a few minutes ago and seconds later Zola just froze. Then you came back out just a few minutes later."

"What?" Jack said looking up at Jal. "That can't be possible. I've been in there for hours. Maybe days."

Jal gave Jack a wide-eyed stare.

"No," she said. "That's impossible. We've only been on Methes for just over an hour. Our fleet was just engaging the Zolanites when we attacked Zola."

"Our fleet!" Jack suddenly remembered. "Bob? Orlo? What happened?"

As if to answer his question he saw the form of a Scalayan diving down through the sky followed by dozens of different ships. He realized it was Zev and there on his back must be UFO Bob!

"We did it," he said softly. "We made it."

His hands began to shake.

And for the second time, the world went dark.

This time when Jack woke up, Mr. Sunshine's ass was not on his face. He was in a soft bed. The air was cool and his cat was curled up next to him.

He didn't raise up from the bed, but turned his head. Through a skylight he could see outside. There was a deep purple sky and he saw Scalayans flying in the distance.

How much time had passed now?

Jack tried to get up without disturbing Mr. Sunshine, but he ruffled the cat. Mr. Sunshine opened his eyes and glared at Jack, stretched, turned over and curled back up again.

His stirring must have alerted someone because a Xanthian entered the room. Though they'd been more than a little off-putting at first, Jack had quickly gotten used to them so they were now only slightly off-putting. But he'd learned many of them were great scientists, doctors and researchers and had been a great asset in the struggle against Zola. They'd also been visiting Earth for some time.

This particular Xanthian, Jack learned, was named Twrrrrg and was a multi-species medical specialist. After some small talk, he gave Jack a quick scan with a few medical devices. Then he did the same to Mr. Sunshine and said both were doing fine.

When Twrrrrg left, Jack found his clothes, the same ones he'd been wearing when he was brought to Scalaya (cleaned of course), and got dressed. Mr. Sunshine seemed perfectly happy staying in bed. Jack realized he was in the same spire where they'd had their original war council. Back in the same room he'd been staying in before in fact. He sat on the edge of the bed for a moment enjoying the peace and quiet. And the fact both he and Mr. Sunshine were alive and well. He was especially enjoying that.

After a bit he left his room and found his friends all gathered in the meeting chamber. The doctor had just told them he was awake.

It was a cheery reunion. They embraced Jack. Slapped him on the back and shoulders repeatedly and talked excitedly about everything that had happened. He learned that, though there had been some deaths among the Methens and the Zolanites, it was mercifully few and, even now, wizards from Scalaya, those who were former followers of Zola who'd stayed around, as well as Xanthian scientists, were resurrecting as many of the dead as they could. Most would be restored either through magic or if that was impractical, by Xanthian scientists who had provided Barry with his artificial body.

Some opted for whatever afterlife their species went to after, well, life. Mostly the ones who would be greeted in the afterlife by a large number of people who definitely weren't virgins. The rest were bound for an afterlife that was nothing more than an eternally quiet afternoon spent reading a good book.

A few, not many, decided they wanted to be ghosts.

Jack was astounded and more than a little confused, but happy to hear things seemed to be returning to whatever passed for normal on both Methes and Scalaya. He was also happy to learn what had actually happened while he was in the temple, but he still wasn't sure why it seemed days had passed for him when it was only minutes for the rest.

Kkkkgh, who had become fast friends with UFO Bob was with them and explained.

"Zola was apparently trying to use a small singularity, what you humans amusingly call a back hole, to enhance her powers enough to resurrect her former familiar in your Mr. Sunshine. It was housed in the temple, though it couldn't be housed in this dimension. The temple entrance was actually a dimensional portal.

"When you entered, you crossed the threshold of a different pocket of the time/space continuum. As you got closer to the singularity, it began to distort your personal time stream. It's also why you felt so much heavier while you got closer."

Jack nodded in a way which indicated he had no clue what Kkkkgh was talking about, but that it didn't matter, because he believed him and that he had no desire to have Kkkkgh try and explain it again in a way in which Jack might be able to understand because there wasn't any way that would work either and they both would just end up frustrated.

That particular nod looks just like an ordinary nod of the head, but with a lot of very subtle subtext. It translates very well to Xanthians.

"But what about this soul thing that's supposedly in my cat?" Jack asked warily, wondering if at some point in the future Mr. Sunshine might be in need of an exorcist.

"Not to worry," Barry said reassuringly. "The fragment of the soul that remained of Utu Lu was minuscule to begin with. In fact, I think it was more of an echo than a fragment. That's why you were able to prevent it from emerging. Even if it ever did emerge again, which would require an even more powerful black hole, I don't think there's enough left to worry about."

Jack nodded in a similar way as before, but this time indicating he gave up on understanding and was actually moving toward regretting asking any questions at all, but still couldn't help himself.

"The one thing I don't understand," Jack said after the nod's meaning had sunk into the rest. "Actually, there's loads I don't understand, but I'm okay with that. But how was Zola actually defeated? And what exactly happened to her?"

"As for the latter," Barry said. "She's in a magically induced paralytic condition."

"What?"

There were no nods in Jack's repertoire that would be an adequate response to this.

"It's complicated," Barry said. "It has to do with the mystical powers which she was attempting to harness…"

"She turned to stone," Jal said, obviously tired of the long, technical explanations.

"Got it." Jack said, relieved that there was some bit of understanding he could finally grasp onto.

"As for why she turned to stone," Barry said. "We're not sure. We just assumed it was something you did. Our battle with Zola wasn't going well. We were holding our own, but that was about it. Our fleet was outnumbered 10 to 1.

"Even with her son, Tenga, and some of his followers turning against her, it wasn't enough."

"All I did was find Mr. Sunshine and then pass out," Jack said. "Unless I did something in my sleep I don't remember."

"Well, I guess we'll never know," Bob said. "Maybe it was Mr. Sunshine."

A chuckle went through the others in the group.

"Well, whatever it was," T'ki said, "it worked. The Methens are free. Zola is no longer a danger and for the first time in many millennia we can live without the shadow of fear hanging over us."

"Sounds like it's time for a party," UFO Bob said.

And there was a party. A tremendous party spanning dozens of star systems, but the focal point of the party started on Scalaya centered around Jack, Bob, Jal, Barry, Orlo, T'ki and Zev. They were superstars. And when they traveled to Methes a few days later, the focus of the party followed them and became even bigger. It seemed like every single Methen came out to greet them. Statues had already been erected to them. Jack was taken aback somewhat by all the attention, but he did really like one statue that showed him in a rather heroic pose with Mr. Sunshine perched on his shoulder, head held high.

One day, during a break in the celebrations while everyone rested and sobered up, Jack snuck away and headed for the former fortress and temple built by Zola. He'd never really gotten a chance to see what had happened to her. He knew she was still there, in the same place where she'd been frozen almost a week earlier.

The entire area had been cordoned off, but fame has its benefits and he had no trouble getting through. He walked across the wide expanse between the two structures toward the solitary figure standing there, now looking pitiably small.

Jack had never seen Zola up close, but given her description he wasn't sure what to expect. Part of him thought she would be some kind of Wicked Witch of the West figure, but what Jack saw was a face that, even in stone, was beautiful.

"I guess I'm not such a silly human now," Jack said, walking around the statue.

There was discussion as to whether Zola was actually dead or if she was just permanently altered in this molecularly-locked form. Jack shuddered to think she might still be alive inside that shell. Conscious and trapped. Evil as she was, it wasn't a fate he would wish on anyone.

"You had so much power," Jack whispered. "You could have done so much with it. So much good."

He moved slowly around the figure, eying it. And for the first time, he felt anger welling up inside.

"You called me pathetic. Well, maybe I seem that way to you. And, maybe I am in some ways, but now look. I was part of the group who defeated you. Maybe a small part, but poor little old pathetic me helped take you down."

He felt a burning inside.

"So what does that make you? Huh? Getting taken down by poor pathetic me.

"And just so you know, my breakup with Maya WAS mutual. I met her when the band she was managing was on tour, but the band broke up and she decided to stick around town for a while. But then the band got together again…"

Jack stopped, realizing none of this was relevant, that his voice was rising in anger, that maybe - just maybe - the breakup had been a little more one sided than he liked to believe. And also that he was talking to a space witch turned into a statute who couldn't actually hear him.

It didn't matter. He leaned in face-to-face with Zola.

"Who's the loser now?"

Jack realized something inside of him had changed. He was definitely no newly-born hero. He was still a guy who sold photocopier paper, but now there was something more…

Oh crap! He suddenly thought. I've been gone at least a week and I didn't call in! And no one knows where I am. And my house is a disaster!

Suddenly, the old Jack rushed back in and his stomach tightened with worry. But then he glanced up at Zola and all of that faded away. He shrugged his shoulders.

"I guess I'll just deal with all that when I get home. No big deal."

And he suddenly realized it actually wasn't a big deal.

As he looked at the form of the former ancient Sumerian sorceress, he felt a rush again. A smile crossed his face and he turned and started walking away. After a few steps, he turned back to Zola.

"Oh, and by the way, *never mess with my cat again!*"

He glared at the unblinking eyes, turned and walked off, in pure Hero Mode - never looking back.

Last

The grass was wet with dew in the field where Jack stood. He placed the carrier with Mr. Sunshine curled up inside onto the ground and looked up as T'ki rose into the distance with the transport pod containing Jal, Barry and Bob in tow. He watched until they disappeared completely and then picked up the carrier and began walking toward home.

Jack wasn't a bit surprised when Bob said he was staying behind. He would work with Barry and the others to rebuild Methes and work with the other worlds to make sure nothing could ever threaten their freedom again.

"I'll come back one day," Bob had told him after he made the decision. "Orlo really wants to see Earth. And so does Barry. Even though it's changed so much, he misses it and wants to see what it's become. He might be a little disappointed.

"I just feel like I should stay here a while. There's so much going on and I really feel like I should be part of it."

He'd tried to talk Jack into staying. They all had. And it was very tempting, but in the end he realized how much he missed home - as dull and uninteresting as it was.

Bob understood and handed Jack a letter. It was to what few family members he had back home explaining he'd gone overseas for a while and he'd get back in touch with them when he returned. He reassured Jack they wouldn't worry about him too much. This wasn't the first time he'd disappeared seemingly off the face of the Earth.

Jack looked down from time to time as he walked and checked on the Mr. Sunshine, still curled up in a ball and occasionally annoyed if the carrier was jarred slightly, but still none the worse for wear. Did he realize he was home? Did he care? Who knows.

He'd been left back in the clearing where they'd all originally left Earth all those days ago, an easy walk home. When he got back to his house it still looked much as he left it, only now with lots of yellow police tape everywhere and little flags and markers in the yard where apparently officials had tried to determine what had happened.

Jack still wasn't sure what he'd tell them. He thought of telling them the truth. Some time locked away in a nice hospital might be a welcome rest, but then, who'd take care of Mr. Sunshine?

When the time came, something would come to him. He was sure of that.

He ignored the yellow tape and walked around the back of the house and into what used to be his kitchen. It was early morning, just beginning to grow light. He decided to pack up a few things for him and Mr. Sunshine, find a nice pet-friendly hotel nearby and then start trying to piece his life back together. Hopefully, he still had a job. After all, there was no one who knew more about photocopier paper than him. If he'd been canned for not showing up for work for a couple of weeks, he'd simply go somewhere else. Maybe back to the city and give it another try.

Jack spent about ten minutes getting things together. The morning light was brighter now making it easier to find things. He had a couple of bags packed and was standing in the living room looking around. He spotted the book he'd been reading the day this all started. It was still lying on the couch, open to the page where he'd stopped.

He picked up the book and then reached over to the nearby table and found a piece of paper to use as a bookmark. He stuck it in the book and started to close it when he noticed what was on the paper. It was a number. A phone number. One he hadn't used in years and wasn't sure why he still had it.

Jack smiled as he looked at the number and made up his mind he was going to call it as soon as he could.

ABOUT THE AUTHOR:

Joseph R Gurner is, to quote the great Douglas Adams, an ape-descended life form who still thinks digital watches are a neat idea.

Beyond that, he's a former grave-digger, recovering journalist, a librarian, a wannabe musician with delusions of grandeur and a life-long resident of Mississippi.

While in his time he's had many cats (and more than a few dogs - plus one pig), he's never had one that was kidnapped by aliens. At least that he's aware of.

www.ingramcontent.com/pod-product-compliance
Lightning Source LLC
Chambersburg PA
CBHW020630250626
47154CB00004B/1746